Veiled Threats

Kate Allenton

Discover other titles by Kate Allenton

At

www.kateallenton.com

ISBN-13: 978-0692528808
ISBN-10: 0692528806

DEDICATION

This book is dedicated all the people who believed in me before I wrote my first word.

ACKNOWLEDGMENTS

I'd like to acknowledge my
READERS....You all rock.
Thank you for taking a chance on my
books.

1 CHAPTER

Aiden Monroe slid the sunglasses over his eyes as he meandered down Main Street. His target was less than twenty five yards ahead. The man rested his palm on the female's lower back, occasionally letting it drift down to her ass. She giggled and batted her eyelashes back at him, ignoring the tourists and residents as they passed by. The woman pulled a compact out of her purse and used the mirror to reapply her cherry-red lipstick. Smooshing her lips together, she blew a kiss. She snapped the mirror closed before whispering into the man's ear. The guy chuckled in response.

Aiden pressed the com in his ear. "I've got visual on our target."

"Copy that," Roman answered. "Hold your position."

Aiden released a pent-up breath. All of the secret conversations and covert planning had brought him to this moment in time. "We should do this now, before they get away."

"Negative," Roman clipped. "We need two more minutes to get into position."

"You're out of time. ETA in five seconds."

"Shit," Roman exclaimed.

"Surprise." A chorus yelled into the earpiece, the tone rendering Aiden momentarily deaf. He yanked the plastic out of his ear, leaving it to dangle on his shoulder by the spiraled cord.

Aiden pulled the door of the restaurant open to find his boss and business partner, Marshall Dixon, and his wife, Sophie, standing inside. A congratulations banner hung along the restaurant wall. Baby blue and pink streamers hung from the ceiling matching the balloons grouped on every table.

Friends and townspeople, dressed in their Sunday best, stood inside prepared to engulf the pair in hugs.

Sophie appeared minutes later by Aiden's side. "You're out of practice. I caught your tail the moment we parked."

"Then I'm not the one slacking, Mrs. Dixon." Aiden grinned, giving himself a mental high five as he tossed his arm around Sophie's shoulders. "You should have caught me well before that."

"I sniffed you out at the end of our driveway," Marshall announced, bursting Aiden's momentary bubble before pulling Sophie away from Aiden. Marshall wrapped his arms around her baby-filled belly.

"Seriously?" Aiden's smile fell.

"Sophie blew you a kiss when she used her mirror to check your location."

Aiden's mouth dropped open. "That was on purpose?"

"Well, she is married to the best." Marshall grinned proudly and took Sophie by the hand, easing her back into the midst of baby shower attendees.

"You must have forgotten to eat your Wheaties this morning," Amber jested in passing.

She glanced over her shoulder. Her

green eyes traveled the length of his body and back up, devouring him like candy by a woman watching her figure. Her eyes sparkled with mischief as her body, draped in a flowered sundress, teased him. Her dark hair was pulled away from her face, giving him full view of the smile on her lips. "I'm not surprised."

"Tease all you want, Ms. Cantrell." Aiden eased closer to her, and taking her by the arm, steered her away from prying ears. "We both know you're happy I'm here."

"Only because I need your help." She glanced back into the room, ushering Aiden farther away from the party and into the cooler.

"Have you received more letters?" he asked.

She pulled an envelope out of a hidden pocket in her dress and handed it to him. "This arrived yesterday. Apparently, whoever's responsible for my little love notes, wasn't scared off."

He opened the note. A chill seeped into his bones, replacing their easy banter.

Time to come home.

Yep, play time was over. Aiden held up

the paper, unease and apprehension washing over him. The letters were coming more frequently, and still Aiden had no clue who was sending them or why. "Who are you hiding from, Amber?"

She glanced down at her feet as if unable to meet his gaze.

He used his finger to lift her chin. "I can't help you unless you tell me."

Her eyes searched his. Questioning what? His sincerity?

"I—"

The cooler door swung open, cutting off her words. Detective Jack Love stood in the doorway. He flashed his badge to Aiden. "Amber, I need you to come with me."

Amber closed Aiden's hand around the letter. Her eyes filled with worry. "Keep this with the others."

He nodded and watched as Jack led her out of the cooler and to the front door. Sophie shot Jack a questioning, and somewhat angry glare, as she watched her ex-boyfriend steering her best friend out the door; her eyes, widened in alarm, whipped back to Aiden's as panic clouded her face.

Before she could demand answers that he couldn't give her, Sophie grabbed her stomach and doubled over as a scream ripped from her lips.

Aiden moved quickly to Marshall's side as he eased his wife down to the floor, the crowd only parting to let the town doctor pass with his medical bag in hand.

One nod from Marshall and Aiden was out the door after Amber. Sophie would send out the hounds of hell to haunt their asses if Marshall or Aiden let anything happen to her best friend. It was a fact and a threat she'd issued more than once.

Aiden slid his phone out of his pocket and dialed his brother, Alexander. He was the only attorney he trusted to get Amber out of whatever mess she'd gotten herself into. "Jack just hauled Amber Cantrell out of Sophie's baby shower with a flash of his badge. I want her released within the hour. Can you manage that?"

"Depends on what they picked her up for. Was she charged with anything? Was she read her rights?"

"No," he answered.

"Good, I'm on my way." The line went

dead.

Aiden started in a jog back to where he'd left his car, breaking the posted speed limit on his way to the station. He'd barely turned off the car when his brother, dressed in an expensive suit, stepped out of his Lexus.

"You were fast," Aiden said in way of greeting.

"I was closer. You must have sped."

Aiden shrugged. So what if he had. He'd have ended up at the same destination and his brother would have bailed his ass out. "Good thing I know an attorney."

Alexander rolled his eyes. "You are an attorney, dumbass."

"Not practicing," Aiden grumbled beneath his breath as they stepped into the police station's empty lobby.

Alexander went into attorney mode, passing the female cop working the front desk his card. He nodded to the closed door and mentioned Amber's name.

Aiden rested his hip against the counter, silently cataloging the names of the deputies on duty. Sophie's brother was at the party, along with his wife, leaving the office short-staffed. Even better for a potential jail break if need be.

The woman took the card before disappearing into the conference room. He glanced at his watch as he tapped the counter in anticipation, curiosity taking a back seat to the worry churning his gut.

Amber was a good girl, albeit flirtatious and sexy. There had to be a reasonable explanation for Jack to haul her away much less crash the party. No. Something was wrong. Aiden could feel it in every fiber of his being. Something was dead wrong.

The deputy working the reception desk walked out of the office with Jack following on her heels.

"Why are you here?" His tone was less than cordial.

"You have my client," Alexander answered.

Jack glanced over his shoulder, scanning the room. "What the hell are you talking about?"

Aiden rested his elbows on the counter, leaning forward. "Amber Cantrell."

Alexander eased his brother back. "What is she being charged with?"

Jack rolled his eyes in frustration. "She's not under arrest, you dipshit," he said, the comment directed straight at Aiden. "And she doesn't need an attorney, Alex. Go home."

Jack turned to walk away when Amber stepped out of the room. Her tear-stained face was flushed;, the humor in her eyes from teasing him at the baby shower was nowhere to be found. Her bottom lip quivered, and another salty tear streaked a trail down her cheek, causing Aiden's heart to plummet. Anger flashed through Aiden. He clenched his fist, determined to get to the bottom of this. He pitied the asshole that had caused her tears. *Just give me a name.*

"Jack...it's okay." Amber's voice was soft, as though she'd been through the wringer. "I want Aiden here."

Jack stepped in front of her and placed his palm on her arm in a gentle caress. "Are you sure about this?"

"Fuck me," Aiden whispered. Jack's gentle touch and serious concern set Aiden's alarms on high alert. Something was going on, and if Jack and the police were involved, it was worse than he'd imagined.

"Come on, Aiden." Jack gestured with his head toward the conference room before leading Amber back inside.

"Call me if you need an attorney." Alexander patted his brother on his back. "Let's hope you don't."

Aiden had barely heard his brother's words as he hurried around the partition that separated the visitors' area from the investigators. Stepping into the conference room, Aiden lifted a brow as he took in the occupants of the room. Two men dressed in business suits sat at the table.

"Aiden, these are Detectives Jim Lawson and Steve Sims."

Aiden gave them a curt nod and moved to Amber's side, turning her to face him. Her bloodshot eyes brimmed with overflowing tears. He leaned down making their eyes level. "You okay?"

She nodded and closed her eyes, allowing another round of tears to fall free. Aiden's heart cracked on the spot. He hated to see women cry. He pulled her into his arms, wrapping her in his embrace, holding her against his chest while stroking her hair, comforting her as best he could.

Her shoulders shook as she let the tears fall freely.

"We'll deal with this. Whatever it is," he whispered into her ear, ignoring the company he was in. "I promise."

"Aiden, it's not what you think," Jack explained, taking a seat at the end of the table.

Amber leaned out of his embrace and swiped at her face before she met his gaze. "My grandmother is missing."

A missing grandmother was one thing. A dead grandmother was another. Investigation was a language he spoke, and he was damn good at his job. The knots in his stomach eased as he pulled her back into his chest. He peered at Jack with a raised brow. "I thought you said she didn't need an attorney."

"She doesn't." Jack leaned back in his chair watching curiously as he spoke. "I'm her alibi."

Well, isn't that just freakin' great? Amber was consorting with assholes now. Had Aiden missed a memo? Last Aiden knew, Jack was dating his sister, Alexis.

Aiden refrained from calling Jack out. This wasn't the time or the place, and if he was Amber's alibi, far be it from Aiden to put a question in the detective's mind.

"I'm afraid our visit is standard procedure. Her name is on our list because she's a relative. We're starting with those that knew her best."

Aiden pulled out a chair and eased Amber into it before taking the seat next to her.

"You're assuming there was foul play," he said more as a statement than a question.

The men exchanged a quick look with each other, confirming Aiden's guess. They opened a file and slid a picture across the table. Amber squeaked and covered her mouth as she picked it up.

"Is that her house?" Aiden asked.

She nodded while fighting the tears, and Aiden slipped the picture from her hand. The coffee table lay on its side, the legs, broken and splintered on the floor nearby. Ceramic knickknacks were shattered into small pieces. Picture frames lay smashed on the ground, and the pictures in the frame were missing.

"Miss Cantrell, can you tell us the last time you talked to your grandmother?"

Amber swiped her tears. "I talked to her two days ago." Amber leaned forward. "You will find her, won't you? Tell me you'll find her."

Aiden stroked Amber's back in a comforting way.

"We will try our best," Sims answered.

"If they don't, I will," Aiden reassured her without thought, not caring if he sounded self-assured. It was the truth.

"What was the nature of your conversation?" Lawson asked. "Did you notice anything out of the ordinary last time you spoke? Anything she said, anyone she complained about? Anything at all you can think of, no matter how small, might help us."

Jack rose from his spot and poured a cup of water, placing it in front of Amber. He rested his hand on her shoulder and gave a gentle squeeze. His considerate move didn't go unnoticed.

"We talk once a week." Amber's hands trembled as she took a sip of her water. "It was mainly routine questions. Am I eating? Am I staying out of trouble? How Sophie was doing with her pregnancy. When will she see me again? The normal stuff a grandmother worries about. Nothing out of the ordinary...except..."

"Except what?"

"She told me about stuff she'd misplaced. She chalked it up to her age, but I'm not so sure that was the case."

"Why do you think that?"

"That woman has the memory of an elephant. She always had, so when she told me she'd misplaced her car keys, along with her purse, I couldn't believe it."

"Was she on any medication?"

"No, not my grandmother. She was healthier than I am. Convinced eating a grapefruit a day, taking her vitamins, and walking kept her that way. She hated when family tried to dote on her and take care of her. It aggravated her."

"Did she say anything else?"

Amber studied her fidgeting fingers, and she squeezed her eyes shut and nodded. "Oh god...Yes, she did."

"What?" Sims prodded.

She lifted her gaze and took a deep, steady breath. "She told me about a call she got from the DA's office."

The detectives shared a concerned look.

"They were trying to reach me." Amber visibly swallowed. "To tell me that Trent Daniels was released from prison."

"Who?" Jack sat forward in his chair.

Amber glanced at Aiden, and his stomach clenched. He now knew the name of the man leaving her notes and what she hadn't told him in the cooler at the restaurant. It now made sense. "You know him?"

She nodded.

"Well, are you going to clue the rest of us in?" Jack grumbled.

"The asshole is leaving her notes." Aiden's jaw twitched as he answered. He pulled the latest note, that she'd wanted him to keep, from his pocket and slid it across the conference table. "She's found them on her car, at her home, everywhere she goes. She's even found one in her purse."

"Have you seen him in town?" Jack asked, pulling his phone from his pocket. He typed ferociously across the keyboard. He paused, waiting for her reply.

"No." She gestured to the note lying on the table. "Not once."

Jack's brow rose, and he continued to type.

"We'll talk to his probation officer, check his address and talk to him next. Do you have a weapon or a way of protecting yourself, Ms. Cantrell?"

"She has a .38 Special. She's been trained in personal self-defense by members at Dixon Security, and she has me," Aiden answered.

Jack chuckled but didn't share what he thought was humorous.

"And what is your relationship to Amber?" Sims asked.

"Great question," Jack said and crossed his arms, that smug smile returning. "I'm dying to hear this."

Amber met their gazes. "We're just friends. We were dancing at the wedding when a waiter gave me the first note."

"He was at the wedding?" Jack's smile slipped.

The other detectives looked confused.

"Amber's best friend, Sophie, married my boss, Marshall Dixon, who owns Dixon Security. She also happens to be the chief's little sister. As you can imagine, the wedding and reception guest list comprised security specialists and police officers."

"Did you get a description from the waiter?" Lawson asked. "And check the surveillance?"

Aiden rested his arms on the conference table. "The waiter never saw the guy. He claims he found the envelope in the kitchen, and the security feed confirms his story. The cameras didn't catch anyone coming or going prior. Whoever did this looped the security feed to replay the hours leading up to the wedding."

"You said this has been going on for months?"

Amber nodded.

"If Trent was just released from prison, how is it possible he left those notes several months ago?"

"It's possible he had an accomplice." Alden suggested.

"What is your connection to Trent?"

Amber closed her eyes and let out a

deep breath before meeting the Lawson's gaze. "He was stalking me and tried to abduct me."

The detectives shared a concerned look. "I assume he didn't get away with it?"

"My uncle is the only reason I'm still alive. He stopped Trent." Her brows pinched.

With Amber's confession, Trent Daniels was just placed at the top of Aiden's most wanted list. If he ever caught this son of a bitch, he'd deal with the low life himself.

"Amber, do you know if Trent Daniels or any of his friends are capable of manipulating the feed?" Lawson asked.

"I don't know," she answered. "You have to understand. I haven't seen him in over nine years. I don't know what he's capable of. I moved the same day he was sentenced for stalking. You don't think..." Amber's voice broke as the detectives rose.

"Was there any blood at the scene," Jack asked.

"No," Lawson answered.

Aiden clasped his hands on the table and leaned forward. These guys were holding back something if they thought foul play was involved and the woman wasn't just on some trip. And it was about time they came clean. "Was her car missing? Did you check her computer? Track her financials or her cell phone?"

Lawson's lips pulled into a fine line before he answered. Yeah, they were hiding something, the question was what. "Her car was in the driveway and her purse was located in her home. None of the contents were missing. Her driver's license, ATM card and even her cell phone were in it." Lawson stood. "Ms. Cantrell, we're doing everything we can to find your grandmother."

Sims pulled out his card. Aiden took it and handed him his. "We'll call you once we locate Trent."

Aiden nodded and rested his hand on Amber's back. "Thank you, Detectives."

Aiden dropped his hand and whispered into Amber's ear, "Wait here."

She sat back down as Aiden followed the detectives out of the office. He stood on the precinct steps and watched them leave in the unmarked car. He pulled out his phone and speed dialed Marshall.

"Speak," Marshall barked. "Sophie is

threatening to leave the hospital and drive to the damn station if I don't give her a report."

"The short version is that Amber is fine, but we have a problem. Her grandmother is missing, and her damn stalker has been released from prison. We're just wrapping up, and I'll bring her to Sophie."

Aiden spun on his heels to head back into the precinct. "We need to run a background on the stalker and get a copy of the police files on the missing grandmother. They aren't telling us something. I can feel it."

"I'll call the office and get them busy. You get Amber here and fast. Sophie's blood pressure is spiking, and I don't think she'll calm the fuck down until she can see that Amber isn't in handcuffs."

"Copy that," Aiden answered and slid the phone back into his pocket.

2 CHAPTER

Aiden scanned the hospital parking lot as he walked Amber inside. The realization they were dealing with a stalker, and now a missing grandmother, had upped the ante and stretched his nerves. It was one thing to be looking out for an ex-boyfriend or admirer, but Aiden had a feeling psychopath might be a better description. Coming to the hospital and being out in the open wasn't an ideal situation for what they were dealing with, but it was a necessity if her presence alone helped Sophie to relax.

"Jack's your alibi?" Aiden asked, giving her a sideways glance.

"There's a lot you don't know about me, Aiden."

"I think the convicted stalker proves that, but I didn't realize you date assholes." He glanced at her again. "I would have pegged you as smarter."

"I'm smart enough to stay clear of you, Mr. One and Done. If I'm ever after an easy lay, I know your number," she tried to lighten the mood. "Besides, I'm not dating Jack."

They took the elevator up to the fifth floor, and he ushered Amber into Sophie's room.

"About time," Marshall grumbled. "I thought I was going to have to come and get her myself."

"James Bond here circled twice to make sure we didn't have a tail." Amber sat on the hospital bed facing Sophie and placed her hand on Sophie's belly. "How is she?"

Sophie smiled. "Better than you. What happened? Do I need to send Marshall to kick Jack's ass? Because I will. You just say the word."

Amber gave her a sad smile. "My grandmother is missing."

"What?" Sophie tried to sit up, but

Amber patted her shoulder and eased her back down.

"When? How?"

"We don't know anything yet." Aiden crossed his arms over his chest and rubbed his chin. "Her house was vandalized, and they can't find her."

Amber rubbed Sophie's belly again. "You don't need to worry about any of this. You need to concentrate on this sweet baby."

"Your grandmother is alive," Sophie blurted out. "I'd have seen her spirit by now, and Will, my guide, just popped in to confirm it."

Sophie's psychic gifts had solved more than one case. Aiden wasn't surprised that they'd proven useful in this one, even from the confines of a hospital bed. The tension in Amber's shoulders deflated, and some of her unvoiced fear cleared from her eyes.

"You might as well tell her the rest while she's at the hospital. It's better here than at her house where the doctors aren't readily available. Both Marshall and Sophie need to know what you're dealing with."

"What?" Sophie asked as Marshall

moved to the other side of the bed, taking his wife's hand.

Amber shot Aiden a scowl over her shoulder. He raised a challenging brow. "Either you tell her or I will."

"Trent was released."

Sophie's eyes grew wide, confirming Aiden's suspicion. Damn, was he the only one kept in the dark? "When?""

"A week ago," Aiden answered.

The beeping on the machine nearby started to speed up. "And you didn't tell me?"

"Calm down, baby," Marshall soothed. "We aren't going to let anything happen to Amber. I promise."

"I didn't want you to worry." Amber's look turned sincere. "I don't even know if he knows where I am, much less whether I'm in town."

"Except for the notes he or his accomplice are leaving," Aiden added, earning him another glare, only this time from Marshall.

"What notes?"

"Someone is leaving her notes," Marshall confirmed. "We're already working on it. It's nothing to get upset about. Aiden is going to figure it out and handle it."

"Are you?" Sophie asked. Her brow hitched. "Do you promise?"

"I promise, Sophie. Amber will be safe with me; we'll catch this creep, and he'll never bother her again."

"You'll make sure?" Sophie asked, now looking up at her husband.

"Of course." Marshall kissed her forehead. "That's why Aiden is here. We're going to go grab some coffee and discuss our next step while you visit with Amber." He rubbed Sophie's arm. "You have nothing to worry about, and neither does she."

Marshall gestured to the door, and Aiden followed him out of the hospital room and toward the elevator. He pressed the button and waited until they were inside before he spoke. "Roman is working on pulling the reports."

Aiden nodded.

"Do you think it's connected?"

"I don't know," Aiden answered honestly. "The police are trying to rule out Amber as a suspect. They always start with the people closest to the victim. They were on a fishing expedition. They wanted to question her alibi and see what she knew. They don't have any idea where her grandma is, only that her house was trashed."

"Did she have an alibi?"

"Yep. You'll never guess who with."

"Jack."

"How did you know?"

Marshall grinned. "She hasn't told you yet?"

"What is up with all these secrets?" Aiden followed Marshall off the elevator and down the corridor toward the coffee shop. "You care to enlighten me?"

"It's not my place." Marshall patted Aiden on the back before grabbing a cup and filling it with coffee. "I want you to stick to Amber like glue."

The assignment wasn't issued out of the blue. Aiden had been going to suggest some type of detail at their next security meeting if he couldn't get a beat on the prick leaving her notes.

"I want you to accompany her to her grandmother's and find what the other investigators missed. Talk to the rest of the family, get the inside scoop, and then do some digging into her past with this stalker. We might as well tackle both issues while we're there."

"I agree."

"Great." Marshall headed toward the elevator, stabbed the button, and they both stepped on.

"You know....if we're dealing with a stalker, maybe we should consider drawing him out."

"Let's see what we can dig up first on the missing grandmother and then we'll deal with catching this asshole. You just make sure you watch her back." Marshall held the elevator door open when it reached Sophie's floor. "You stick to her like fucking glue. Got me?" Marshall placed his hand on Sophie's door and paused. "If Sophie gets upset, then I'll get upset, and no one wants that."

Following Marshall into the room, Aiden spotted his new best friend. Amber was seated on the bed where they'd left her.

The door opened behind them, and the doctor walked in with his clipboard in hand.

"If you'll excuse us, I need to examine Mrs. Dixon."

Amber hugged Sophie and stood. "I'll check in on you later."

Sophie squeezed Amber's hand, and silent girl communication passed between them before they let go.

Aiden placed a kiss on Sophie's forehead before leaning in to whisper in her ear. "I'll take care of her, I promise."

"I'll send you over what you need," Marshall called out after them. "Where will you two be staying, Aiden?"

"Where will who be staying?" Amber spun around to face them both.

"We're staying at my place tonight and taking the jet in the morning."

Marshall nodded in agreement.

"Where will who be staying?" Amber asked again as Aiden ushered her out of the room.

"Us." He grinned and tossed his arm around her shoulder. "You're stuck with me like white on rice while we go back to your hometown to find your Grams and catch this asshole. Marshall's orders."

"Marshall isn't my boss." Amber

stopped dead in her tracks, crossing her arms over her chest. Defiance flashed in her eyes.

"Afraid you don't have a say in it. Look at it this way. You're saving Sophie from the added stress. She'll be worried about your safety otherwise, which means Marshall will be worried. This way, everyone wins."

Amber rolled her eyes. "Everyone except for me."

****

Aiden checked Amber's house before following her into the bedroom to wait for her to pack. He strolled around the light and airy girly room and then picked up the picture sitting on her dresser of Amber and an older lady. "Is this your grandmother that you've told me about?"

Amber slipped the picture out of his hand as tears gathered in her eyes. "Yeah, that's us at the cabin. My grandmother said it was her favorite picture and gave me a copy when I moved."

"We're going to find her," Aiden said reassuringly.

"I know." Amber grabbed the suitcase from her closet, started throwing clothes inside, and laid the picture on top. "She's a strong woman."

Aiden grinned. "You must get it from her."

She disappeared into the bathroom, came out with a bag of toiletries, and tossed them on top. "She raised me when my parents were killed."

"I bet you were a hellion."

Amber smiled as Aiden leaned against her dresser. "I'm sure I was a saint compared to you."

"What happened to your parents?"

"They died in a house fire seventeen years ago when I was ten. It was ruled arson, but they never caught the person responsible."

Aiden mulled that information around in his mind. Had it been her stalker? Was it possible that this guy was a lot more deadly than they were assuming? "Did they have any suspects?"

Amber zipped up her suitcase and chewed her bottom lip before answering him. "Not that they'd tell me."

"You think it was the stalker?"

"Oh God, no. Trent didn't show up until high school. He was like a bad habit I couldn't get rid of. We went on one picnic at the park and he told me he loved me. I realized he was missing a few screws. After I broke things off, he started calling fifty times a day. When that didn't work, he started emailing me and was just a pain in the ass and..."

Her words trailed off as she stared at the blank wall. She shook her head. "He was just a pain in the ass. I wish I'd never gone on that date. I knew better. My gut screamed no, and I didn't listen."

"When did things change?"

"First, things went missing, and he'd leave me notes. When I didn't respond, it moved on to more physical things. My tires were slashed; my windshield was broken; even my locker was vandalized. He'd stand outside my house just watching, but he scared me enough that I couldn't leave my house. We were granted a restraining order, but that didn't stop him. He still showed up but would disappear anytime we called the cops. My senior year was supposed to be the best time of my life, but he ruined it for me. I missed my prom, my senior trip, hell, even my graduation because I was scared. It was like I was a prisoner in my own home while he was off scot-free. My grandmother was the one that researched the stalking laws and kept track of everything. Then one day he made a mistake." She visibly swallowed. "He caught me off guard, stuck a knife to my throat and tried to abduct me. My uncle stopped him, and he didn't get away that time. That put the nail in his coffin."

"How long did he get?"

"Well, it was supposed to be ten years, but it's only been nine. So I guess he got out for good behavior."

"If he's only been out of jail a couple weeks, then it can't be him leaving the notes. They started ten months ago, at the wedding."

"I know." Amber hoisted her bag to land on the floor and rolled it behind her down the hall. "That's why I didn't tell you about him. He was locked up at the time, and besides....he doesn't know where to find me."

"Any other lunatics you're hiding?"

She patted his shoulder. "I can't help it; I'm so lovable."

"I don't know. I haven't seen that side of you yet."

"I only bring her out on special occasions."

Aiden chuckled but kept his comment to himself. Even if Trent wasn't responsible, Aiden wasn't ruling him out. Just because Trent wasn't the one leaving messages didn't mean he wasn't orchestrating the harassment. Aiden pulled out his phone and shot off a text to Marshall to pull the file on the fire to go along with all of the other information he'd need. What had started out as an anonymous note, delivered at the wedding, had now grown into a missing person's case. The coincidences were mounting.

"Do you have everything you need? You aren't forgetting your mood pills, are you?"

"I'm naturally happy...most of the time. Only certain people bring out the worst in me." She grinned, picked up her purse and glanced at the contents before nodding and glancing around her living room one last time. "You know, I've changed. I'm not that scared little girl anymore. I can handle this myself, especially now."

Aiden scanned the street and neighbors, watching for anyone and anything suspicious as he unlocked her car door and let her slide inside. "Just because we trained you to shoot, and taught you how to protect yourself, it doesn't mean you have to do it alone."

"Aiden, there's something else you should know about me...before we take this trip down memory lane. The reason Jack was my alibi..."

He should have told her that her personal life was her own business, but curiosity got the better of him. If Jack had been screwing Amber and cheating on Alexis, it wouldn't dissuade Aiden from helping her, but damned if he'd be quiet and not tell his sister of the asshole's cheating ways. "You're sleeping with him?"

Her lips parted and she stared at him, unmoving. When she snapped her lips closed, she reached into her purse. He paused for a brief second, thinking maybe he'd really pissed her off and she was going for the gun. He stilled her hand in the purse. "Shooting me won't solve your problems."

"You're an asshole." She shook her head, slid her fingers out of her purse, and held up her badge. "I'm not sleeping with him. I'm working with him. Before the wedding, I'd started taking courses at the college to get certified. I just graduated and they hired me. Jack is my field training officer. That's why he's my alibi. I've been training with him for the last two weeks."

Aiden's brow furrowed as he stared at the badge. "You're a cop?"

She grinned. "That's why I said you didn't have to go. I can handle it myself."

Aiden shook his head and shut her door, walking around to the driver's side to slide behind the wheel. He shoved the key in the ignition and turned it. "Just because you carry that badge doesn't mean you have the experience to solve this case. You're still a rookie."

"And you're still an ass."

3 CHAPTER

Amber followed Aiden into his apartment. Hardwood covered the floors of the living room, and everything was neat and tidy, unlike the empty pizza boxes and beer cans she'd been expecting from the bachelor. His off-white walls held a hint of personality with perfectly staged pictures that complemented his furniture. A few magazines were strategically fanned out on the coffee table. A bar separated the kitchen from the living room. The counter was empty and devoid of clutter. No dirty dishes in the sink, not even a cereal bowl from breakfast.

"Nice place, can I get the name of your maid?"

He glanced over his shoulder and grinned. "I don't have one."

"Oh, you must be one of those OCD types. Either that or you don't spend much time here." She grinned and followed him down the hall into the first bedroom. "I'm guessing the latter."

"I can assure you, I'm neither," he answered and hefted her suitcase on top of the perfectly made up bed. The room was like the rest of the house, void of knickknacks or anything personal. Tan walls sported a single painting of flowers on the wall above a cherry dresser. The matching cherry bed had a tan comforter with four fluffy, overstuffed pillows that looked as if it had never been used. Cream curtains hung over the window for privacy.

"Interior decorator?"

Aiden rested his hands on his hips and glanced around the room as if seeing it for the first time. "How'd you guess?"

She gestured to the painting. "You aren't a flowers type of guy. Where's your room?"

He grinned. "Why? Are you going to sneak in later and have your wicked way with me?"

"If I'd wanted that, I would have batted my eyes at you a year ago." She chuckled. "I guess that was another thing Sophie didn't tell you. I've sworn off men." She spun around on her heels and went exploring the rest of the apartment. If she was stuck with him, she figured she'd use her power of annoyance until he was ready to pawn her off on someone else.

"You shouldn't go in there," Aiden called after her.

"Why? Are you afraid you left your handcuffs out?" She opened a door, and her grin grew. Aiden's room was messy, just like she'd expected the rest of the house to be. Dirty clothes hung half in and half out of a hamper in the corner of the room. The unmade bed looked comfortable and well broken in. Even his dresser drawers weren't shut all the way.

She plopped down on the bed and rested her hands behind her head. "Now this is the Aiden I know."

He stood in the doorway with a scowl on his face, and she laughed while leaning up to rest on her elbows.

"Are you always this pushy?"

She grinned. "It's a gift. People either love me or hate me."

He grumbled beneath his breath and walked out of the room.

She scooted off the bed and followed him into the kitchen. "There's still time to back out. Honestly, I don't need a babysitter. I know I got all emotional at the precinct, but I can find her without your help. So how about we tell Sophie that I pulled a fast one and left you here? I could leave you cuffed to the bed. They'd totally buy that." She smiled. "No one would be the wiser."

He grabbed two beers from the fridge and handed her one. He looked as if he was thinking about her offer as he twisted off the top and took a long pull. "There's only one thing wrong with your plan."

"Yeah, what's that?" She tried twisting the lid, only to have the little grooves on the top dig into her hand, leaving an indentation when it wouldn't budge. He took it from her, opened the beer, and passed it back.

"No one is going to buy the story that you pulled a fast one on me. I don't get cuffed to the bed. I do the cuffing; and besides, you need me."

She rolled her eyes and took a drink of the liquid, thankful for the cool reprieve while standing next to Aiden imagining those pretend cuffs dangling from his fingers. She froze.

Oh no, no, no... Aiden is off limits, she chided herself, pushing all thoughts of Aiden out of her mind. She licked her lips to catch the drop of beer and met his gaze. "I don't need you."

He'd zoned in on her tongue, his look unreadable. His eyes darkened to an emerald shade of green before he cleared his throat. For a second, she thought he might pull her into his arms and give her a kiss that was guaranteed to stop time. Not happening. She shoved the thought away, to be buried six feet under.

"Keep telling yourself that." Aiden's smile turned predatory as he walked away, leaving her standing in the kitchen. "Make yourself at home. I need to pack," he called out over his shoulder, but he stopped in the hallway, turning. "Don't think about running. I'll know if you do. I reset the security system after we walked in."

He spun around again and walked away, leaving her to deal with her sexual frustration. Her self-imposed sexual frustration. For the last nine months she'd been meeting with him. Every time a note popped up, they'd meet in secrecy to try and figure things out. He was a natural born flirt and charmer. He probably didn't even realize he'd been tempting her since Sophie's wedding. "I'm an idiot." She leaned against the counter and took another swig of her beer, hoping that it would drown out her heated thoughts. Amber pulled out her phone and shot off a text to Sophie, the only other person in existence who might understand her frustration.

Why him?

Why not him? What did he do now?

He's arrogant, and sexy, and I'm ready to kill him. Couldn't Marshall pair me with someone else...less attractive!!!!!

Sophie fired back several emoticons

with an angel halo over a smiling face. *I trust Aiden. Let him help you*.

Amber's fingers hovered over the letters, knowing if she said no, then Sophie would be worried even more.

For me?

Fine. But I can't promise he'll come back in one piece. Amber ended the text with several of the same emoticons, including a red smiling face with horns.

I'll take what I can get. Are you sure you don't need me to go with you? Or Marshall?

Nope. You rest. I'll be back before my goddaughter makes her grand appearance.

Be safe. Love you.

You too.

Amber slid her phone into her pocket and glanced around the sterile room. She zoomed in on his hanging pictures and debated long and hard about testing her OCD theory and nudging them off center. She grinned and abandoned the thought. Spinning around, she checked his fridge, not surprised to find it bare of sustenance. She let out a sigh and checked to see if his cabinets were in the same predicament. As wonderful as a meal of oatmeal was in the morning, there was no way in hell she'd be eating it for dinner. She flipped out her phone, hit the speed dial to her favorite pizza joint and placed her order, telling the man on the other end to hang on a minute, she leaned into Aiden's room, pausing when she found him standing in his boxers, and damned if she could find her voice.

He turned to face her, a grin stretched across his face. "Did you need something?"

Good God. Aiden had a body made for sin. She swallowed around the lump in her throat and licked her dry lips. "I need your address for pizza delivery."

"555 31st Street, Apartment 3B."

She repeated it into the phone, taking one last glance down his body and back up before turning to walk away.

"Thirty minutes," the guy on the other end answered before saying good-bye.

"It'll be here in thirty minutes," she hollered to him, not wanting to tempt her restraint for not jumping him. "You care if I take a shower?"

Aiden stepped out into the hall. His jeans were pulled up but not buttoned. "Have at it. Towels are under the sink in your bathroom. Do you need me to wash your back?"

Amber rolled her eyes when all she really wanted to do was say, yes, yes, yes. "Nope. I can manage."

He held her captive with his heated gaze and advanced like a predator. He moved in so close he had her pressed against the hallway wall. "When you saw me in my boxers, your look turned hungry, and not for pizza."

Her heart raced in her chest as butterflies took flight. "You wish."

He ran his finger down her neck, and she fought her reaction.

"You're right. Those handcuffs sound pretty good right about now," he whispered as he leaned in. "Unlike you, I'm not afraid to admit we have chemistry. Denying it won't make it go away."

"Unlike you, I can control myself." She slipped out from beneath his arm and disappeared into her room.

"Keep fooling yourself, sweetheart," he called out as she closed the door. She pressed her back to the wood and heard him whistle as he walked away.

"Self-centered, arrogant..." She cussed beneath her breath as she yanked the zipper opening her suitcase "Asshat. Gah." She clenched her teeth together.

She grabbed her toiletries and clothes and stomped to the bathroom, slamming the door. She needed a shower all right, a cold shower to knock some sense into her mind and to cool her body.

He was wrong. It wasn't inevitable, and she was going to prove it to him. More importantly, she was going to prove it to herself. She had more self-control than anyone was giving her credit for, and she'd prove them all wrong. She wasn't going to let one sexy, arrogant man prove her otherwise.

After her shower, she took out the clothes she'd wear tomorrow, changed into her nightclothes, and repacked her toiletries. She stayed busy in her room looking for anything and everything to keep her busy until she heard the doorbell ring.

She walked out to find Aiden had already made two plates and poured their drinks.

"Have a seat." He gestured toward the

table. "You're my guest."

"I'm your assignment. Let's call it what it is."

"We've got lots to talk about." He followed her to the table and pulled out her chair. She eased into it, keeping a skeptical eye on her host.

"No, we don't." She watched him as he placed her plate and drink in front of her before taking his own seat.

"Sure we do." He took a bite of his pizza. "You can start by telling me why you swore off men."

Amber almost spit out her drink, covering her mouth with her hand as she swallowed. "You're kidding, right?"

"I can see where you might think that I'm kidding, but I'm serious," Aiden answered, swiping his mouth with his napkin.

She folded her hands in her lap, ignoring her plate. "I want more." She shrugged, hoping her answer would make the electricity between them fizzle out and die a slow death. "I want the white picket fence, the husband, and the kids. It's that simple. All of the guys I've dated up until now weren't husband material."

Aiden's lips twisted into a smile. "You're looking for a husband?"

"Yep." She raised her brow. "And we both know you're the least likely candidate. So let's keep it simple between us. We're not having sex...Ever."

"Ever is a mighty long time," Aiden challenged.

"Yes...it is," she agreed and took a bite of her pizza, glad that the conversation of her sex life was over.

He took another bite of his pizza and sat quietly for several minutes. "I concede. First things first. We find your grandmother and figure out who's trying to get your attention with the notes."

Aiden's security system beeped, and the door opened. Roman smiled as he shut the door behind him. "You've had a complicated life, Amber Cantrell."

"Oh?" Her brow rose.

"A house fire, a stalker, love notes, and now a missing grandmother." He walked over to the table and dropped the manila files down on top before tossing the backpack strapped to his arms over to

Aiden. "And now, on top of all of that, you have to work with Aiden and you got the unlucky draw of having Jack as a training partner. Someone needs to find you a four leaf clover or something."

"Bite me." Aiden chuckled and unzipped the bag. His eyes widened at the contents before he glanced up at a smiling Roman.

"You're going to need it."

He re-zipped it and dropped the bag by his feet before grabbing the files while Roman fixed a plate, grabbed a beer from the fridge, and then joined them at the table. "Got any suspects?"

"Several," he answered and twisted off the top on the beer. "The uncle has gambling debts. His ex-wife is having an affair with a married man, and two of her cousins, Maria and Bree, wanted to have her grandmother sent to a nursing home so they could get their hands on her house. It seems developers have been after the property and she's the last holdout."

"What!" Amber's eyes widened into saucers. "She never told me that."

Roman shrugged. "The claims against her sanity were withdrawn. So nothing ever came of it."

"That was quick work."

Roman grinned around his pizza. "It's my job, sweetheart. Lucky for you, we're not stopped by red tape. A quick call to one of our contacts and I knew every sordid detail. I also hear you're looking for a husband."

Her cheeks heated at the claim. "Is that in one of your files?"

"Nope." He took a swig of beer. "Beau told me that was why you dumped him."

"I thought he broke up with you," Aiden asked with a tilt of his head.

She just grinned without replying.

"You two should date," Aiden announced, wiggling his finger between them both.

Roman didn't say anything, just looked at her with a raised brow, as if that was his way of agreeing or asking.

"Let's focus on my grandmother first." She gave a polite smile to Roman. "Not that I don't want to date you. You seem like a nice guy."

"I'm not." Roman rose, taking his slice of pizza with him as he headed toward the door. He pulled it open and looked back. "I'll call you when you're back. You can pick the restaurant and we'll celebrate your new job." He gave her a sly wink and disappeared out the door.

"How is it that everyone knew about your job but me?" Aiden asked.

"If I had to guess, Sophie told him, or maybe he found out when he was looking into my file. Why did you try and set me up with Roman?"

"He's a good guy and one of the few I trust. If you're dead set on getting married, it might as well be to one of us."

"You can't control my life." Amber chuckled. "We aren't in some super-secret club or cult where I have to marry within. You guys are too dangerous. Maybe I'm looking for someone more...stable, like an accountant or something."

"You'd be divorced in a year." Aiden rose from his seat and cleaned his spot. "Get some rest, Amber. We've got a long day tomorrow."

He grabbed the files off the table, reset the security code, and headed to his room. "Let me know if you want to snuggle," he called over his shoulder and chuckled as he shut his door.

4 CHAPTER

Aiden slid the sunglasses down over his eyes, blocking the glare of the afternoon sun as he stepped off the last step of the plane. He gazed around at the empty airfield. He'd read the file last night so he knew the small town he was walking into. The only thing he couldn't figure out was why a big developer wanted the property.

"Welcome to Polk, North Carolina, population 5,032." She chuckled and glanced back at him. "When I left, they had to change the number on the sign."

"That narrows down our suspects considerably." He grinned and grabbed the bags as the pilot handed them from the belly of the plane. "If we rule out the kids, I'm sure it will be even less."

Aiden headed toward the SUV parked in front of the only building on the airstrip.

"How did you arrange transportation? When I left, we didn't even have a car rental place. If your car was broken, you walked or asked a neighbor."

"I know people," he answered, opened the driver's side door, and reached beneath the seat, pulling out a set of keys.

"Of course you do," she answered, tossing her bags in the back seat and sliding into the passenger side. "Where are we going to start?"

"First, we're going to check in at the only bed and breakfast this town has, and then we're going to your grandmother's before we go to the police station."

"Why wouldn't we go there first?"

He gave her a sideways glance and slid the key into the ignition and turned it. "We're keeping the element of surprise. Right now we have the upper hand. No one knows you're here, and we've got work to do."

"When did you make reservations at Milly's place?"

He grinned. "Sophie did it for us. Wasn't that sweet of her?" He glanced in Amber's direction, and his eyes twinkled. "The reservation was included in the files that Roman dropped off. They're expecting newlyweds, Aiden and Amber Monroe. We'll be able to kill two birds with one stone. We can draw Trent out of the shadows and maybe confuse your relatives. Maybe they'll tell us something that will help."

Amber rested her head against the seat and closed her eyes. She was going to kill Sophie for guaranteeing that, as newlyweds, they were going to share the same room. Jeez. She gritted her teeth.

"Don't worry. I'm not suggesting we actually make it legal and get married like Marshall and Sophie did for their cover. No one will be the wiser, and you'll get to wear Sophie's ring with the tracker in it that you love so much."

Aiden slid the obnoxiously large ring out of his shirt pocket and handed it to her. "Look at it this way. It's your first undercover job. You can even put the ring on yourself."

"Fine," she grumbled and slid the ring on. She reached over and cupped his face, turning his to meet hers. "Since we're doing this, I guess we should get this over with."

She tilted her head and pressed her lips to his in an effort to get used to his touch, to his taste, to his hungry mouth. When he reached for her to draw her closer, she broke the kiss. Her heartbeat quickened. Her breaths came out in slow pants as her brows dipped. She'd wanted to hate the feeling, to prove that there was no chemistry, and all it did was prove she was dead wrong.

"That didn't suck." Aiden smiled.

Even if it didn't, she'd never tell him. One word of encouragement and he'd up the ante. She knew his type, and she was breaking free from his type. So, instead, she rolled her eyes and righted herself back in the seat, pulling the seatbelt across her body. Her fingers fumbled fastening it into place.

"You're acting nervous." He put the car in drive and started out onto the two-lane road with her pointing out the directions. "You can't act that nervous when I touch you for the first time." He shot her a sideways glance. "It will ruin our charade."

"I'll be fine." She turned toward the window, watching the trees on the lonely strip of road that led into town. "You know, you could have found another cover." She turned to look at him. "One that didn't include all of this." She raised her hand, giving him a good glimpse of the wedding ring on her finger.

He lifted a brow. "I didn't choose this cover, darling. You can thank your best friend for that."

Oh, she certainly would. Just as soon as they had cell service, she was going to blow up Sophie's phone.

Amber pointed out the directions, taking him on the outlying roads to avoid downtown Main Street in an attempt to keep their presence quiet just a little bit longer. Main Street was still in walking distance, but at least they didn't have to drive right through the center of town. He pulled into the parking lot beside the Victorian-style, three-story B&B and killed the ignition, not moving to get out of the SUV.

"Amber..." He turned to look at her. "Everything I do is to keep you safe." The look in his eyes turned sincere. "I'll be a perfect gentleman behind closed doors, but in public... We're going to need to play the part. I'll try to keep my affection to a minimum so that you're not uncomfortable."

"You sound like you've given this speech before."

Aiden smiled. "I've never played husband."

"I can tell." She pressed her lips together. "Aiden, my grandmother means the world to me. She's the most important person in my life, and if that means that I have to play the role of a loving wife to find her, then so be it."

"Atta girl. Now let's go shake some trees and see what falls loose." He stepped out of the SUV and gave a good look around before grabbing both of their bags in one hand. He placed his other hand on the small of her back as he led her up the short walkway toward the door. She opened the door, and they were greeted by a woman Amber's age, with an apron tied around her neck, covered in flour. The name Milly was scrawled across the fabric.

Milly squealed. Amber squealed, and then they flung themselves at each other. Milly and Amber were both talking so fast he could barely keep up.

"Oh my God, you look great."

"So do you."

"I can't believe you got married."

"I know, right?"

Those were the only parts of the conversation he heard while the two friends played catch-up until they decided they needed air and took a breath.

"You can't tell anyone I'm here. It's a surprise."

"My lips are sealed." Milly glanced up at Aiden. "You must be the husband."

"That I am," Aiden answered.

Milly reached behind the counter and grabbed a key with a heart keychain attached to it. "Don't worry. You have the entire top floor to yourself for the next three days. So you can get as loud as you want." She winked at Amber. "I haven't scheduled anyone else in the other rooms up there."

"Thanks. We'll try to keep it down." Amber moved to stand by Aiden, tossed her arm around his waist, and leaned her head on his shoulder.

"It's so great to have you back." She waved her hand and glanced back the way she'd come. "I have to get back to the kitchen. Breakfast is served before ten, lunch around noon, and then, of course, dinnertime starting at six, which is our busiest time. So if you plan to eat here, I'll reserve you a table in the corner for some newlywed privacy."

"Thanks." Amber rested her hand on Aiden's rock-hard chest. Her fingers played with the fabric. "We're just going to get settled and then go find my relatives."

Milly's smile fell. "I'm so sorry about your grandmother, Amber. I can't believe she's missing. I'm sure they'll find that she went to the woods camping or something. Everyone in town is keeping an eye out for her."

"Thank you."

"Did she camp often?" Aiden asked.

"Oh yeah. She and her posse from the Red Hat Society in town take the trails up the mountain once a month to camp. My grandmother, Addie Mae, always comes back with some of the greatest stories."

"Did they check that area and talk to all the members?"

"As far as I know, they got a search team together and scoured the area."

"Thanks." Amber pointed toward the stairs. "We're going to get settled. I appreciate your help."

"Let me know if you need anything. We don't have room service here, but I'd make an exception for you two. I'm so glad you're back."

The women hugged, and Amber led the way up the stairs until they reached the top floor.

"She was chatty."

Amber shoved the key into the door and unlocked it, stepping inside to let him pass before she closed it.

"She was homecoming queen and voted most popular and most likely to succeed."

Aiden grunted, stopping just inside the doorway. There was a small sitting area with tables and a couch along with a king-sized bed pressed up against the wall. The room was perfect, just big enough for their needs without having to be on top of each other.

She moved into the room, tossed her purse down on the bed, and turned back to find him standing in the doorway. "What were you expecting? A heart-shaped, vibrating bed."

He grinned. "With mirrors on the ceiling, complimentary handcuffs, and an extra-large box of condoms in the drawer. I even brought spare change for the timer on the bed."

She smiled and moved to the window, pulling the curtain back for a better view of the town she'd left behind. "Afraid to disappoint you. You won't find any of that stuff here, at least not where others can see. That's taboo."

He hefted the luggage onto the bed and moved to stand behind her, wrapping his arms around her waist.

She stiffened in his embrace.

"You can't make this reaction in public."

She let out a breath and relaxed into his hold.

"Much better." He leaned down and kissed her cheek. "Public displays of affection are inevitable if we're going to sell it."

"You mean like this?" She turned in his hold, wrapped her arms around his neck, and pulled his face down to hers, leaning into him and letting their bodies contour together.

"Kiss me." Aiden's eye color swirled to the dark green she'd seen before. His demand was a whisper between them.

She stilled the butterflies in her stomach and softened her gaze. "Why would I? We don't have an audience."

"Practice." He closed the gap between them and pressed his lips to hers in a heated kiss. His hands, resting on her sides, pulled her closer until she melded with his body as his tongue vied for entrance.

She opened, letting him in, and moaned as he held her. His fingers splayed against her back, caressing and touching her as she let herself enjoy what he offered. She melted in his arms. Her resolve was broken.

His fingers moved up her back and held her close. He broke the kiss. "That's the way a wife would react."

"That's the way a husband would kiss."

"That was the first of many, darling." He released her and put some much-needed breathing room between them. "Now grab your gun and let's go find your grandmother so I can get you the hell out of this town."

Her heart raced in her chest. Her panties had grown damp from just his kiss. She needed to find her grandmother and fast, before she fell hard for Aiden and he broke her heart. Damn Sophie for trying to play matchmaker.

Amber grabbed her purse and the room key and followed Aiden down the stairs. He slid his fingers through hers as they left the house.

By the time they got in the SUV, her body had cooled and her resolve was firmly back in place. She pointed the way to her grandmother's house, the same house she'd grown up in.

Sitting in the driveway, she looked up at the house. It looked smaller than she remembered as a child. The two-story house had been weathered by age, the wood and paint peeling on the exterior. The shrubs were overgrowing, and the grass could have stood a good mowing.

"You okay?" Aiden asked while scanning their surroundings.

"Yeah, it just looks different."

Aiden gave a slow nod.

"I stayed away too long." She pushed the door open and got out. If she'd been closer, if she'd known what her grandmother had been dealing with, she could have put a stop to anyone out to harm her. She had to be the worst granddaughter in the history of granddaughters.

Aiden met her around the front of the SUV. "You couldn't have known something was going to happen to her."

He linked their fingers and walked up the old stairs to the screen door that was covered by crime scene tap.

"I should have known." She pulled the tape free and found the emergency key stashed beneath the loose wooden plank. Unlocking the door, she shoved the key back into its hiding place. Resting her hand on her stomach to stop the butterflies, she stepped into the living room.

Some of the broken stuff still lay on the floor. Fingerprint dust remained on the window frames and door. The room was still in disarray, even though they'd taken pictures. No one had bothered to tidy things behind them.

Amber reached for the nearest table, intent on flipping it over when Aiden stopped her. He shook his head. "We're just here to look."

She nodded and stepped over some of the broken furniture.

"What picture was in this frame?" Aiden asked, pointing down to a broken frame, the glass shattered around it.

"The same one I showed you at my apartment. That was a picture of my grandmother and me at a log cabin my grandpa built on the lake. We used to vacation there when I was little, but after my parents died, Grams said it was too painful."

Aiden moved farther in the room.

"Put your hands were I can see them," a voice growled from the doorway, a familiar voice she hadn't heard in years.

Amber turned in place to find a shotgun pointed at Aiden.

"Amber, what are you doing here?" Her uncle lowered his gun.

"We should be asking you the same thing," Aiden crossed his arms over his chest.

Amber rested her palm on Aiden's arm. "Uncle Stan. I heard what happened. Why didn't someone call me?"

"We didn't know where to find you. She never told us." Uncle Stan walked into the room. "I make it a point to watch the place since the break in happened." Sadness filled his eyes. "She wouldn't want anything else destroyed."

"Are you the uncle who stopped Trent?" Aiden asked.

"Who's this?" Stan asked, ignoring Aiden's question.

"My husband, Aiden Monroe."

He turned his attention back to Aiden. "Yeah, I stopped that piece of shit from taking her. I should have killed his sorry ass while I had the chance."

Aiden offered his hand. "Thank you."

Stan shook it, and his lips twitched. "You're welcome, son. Welcome to the family. Her granny didn't tell any of us she'd gotten married."

"Yeah, well....that's a new development. She didn't know," Amber mumbled, walking away and down the hall toward the rest of the rooms. She stopped in front of her grandmother's room. The bed was meticulously made, everything on the dresser left in its place. The only thing missing, as far as Amber could tell, was the vitamin dispenser that her grandmother kept by the bed.

She walked into the bathroom. It looked untouched. She glanced at the empty hanger on the back of the door. Her favorite robe was missing. Amber walked into the closet, looking for the robe. She'd given to her grandmother last year when she'd come to visit Amber during Christmas. Her grandmother had boasted that the terry cloth robe was her favorite. It wasn't in the closet either. Was it possible her grandma had taken a trip? Had she not even been home when her house was ransacked? The police wouldn't have known to look for the missing items.

Amber returned to the living room to find the atmosphere thick with tension.

"What's going on?"

"Your husband here was asking if I'd seen Trent. Has he been released?"

"Yep. They let him out about two weeks ago," Amber supplied, walking to Aiden's side. She wrapped her arm around his waist. "Uncle Stan, do you know why Maria and Bree were trying to get Grandma committed into a nursing home?"

"A lot has changed since you left. She's getting old. They thought she needed to be around others her age and she refused to go. They considered taking things to court, but they dropped the idea when Grams said they were cut from her will and she wasn't going to put them back in if they continued their shenanigans."

"And you don't think she was getting old?" Aiden asked.

"No, not her. She's as fit as a fiddle, and there was no way in hell she'd leave her home. Not when things were getting hot and heavy between   Doc Shelton and her."

"Oh." Amber grinned. "Was it serious?"

"Serious enough. I came over on Sunday, like I do every week when she makes her famous pancakes, and the doc was sitting at the table in nothing more than a pair of boxer shorts and a smile."

"She doesn't sound like a woman who can't take care of herself." Aiden chuckled and tugged Amber closer, kissing the top of her head.

"As I hear it, the good doc was trying to talk her into selling her property to the developers and to move in with him."

"She said no?"

"Of course she said no. That strong-headed ox would never rely on any man to take care of her. She's stubborn like that. Next thing I knew, she'd kicked his ass to the curb."

"Aw, baby. Now I know where you get it from."

"Shut up." Amber playfully hit Aiden's stomach.

"Do you know what the developers are planning to do with the land?" Aiden asked.

"I've heard all kinds of rumors. At one point, they were going to build a theme park, and another is they were going to set up oilrigs. It's anyone's guess. Since they don't own the land, they haven't applied for any permits."

"Do you know what company?"

"No, but I'm sure Mayor Tinsdale probably knows, if you want to ask him."

"I think we'll do just that. Thanks." Amber hugged her uncle and headed for the door.

"Amber, since Trent was released, maybe you two should stay with me. This house isn't exactly safe."

Aiden patted the man on the back. "We've got accommodations. Keep your eye out for Trent. I'm sure he'll come looking for her."

He nodded. "You take care of my niece."

"I will."

Amber slid into the SUV and was buckling her belt when Aiden got in. She waited until he started the ignition and was headed out on the main road back into town before she spoke. "Grams took her vitamins and her robe. I'm not sure she's actually missing and not just taking an impromptu vacation somewhere."

Aiden's mouth parted and he looked her

way. "Seriously?"

Amber grinned and nodded. "The police wouldn't have known to look for those things, but I did."

"Maybe Trent being released scared her and she decided to leave until the coast was clear. We'll check the paperwork in the police file when we get to the hotel and see if the cops were already looking into her financials. Maybe the use of her credit cards or an ATM can give us an indication of where she was headed."

"I don't know why she left, but I'll feel better when we find her. I think we need to talk to the mayor and the good doctor. I bet if anyone knows where she went, it's the doctor or her best friend, Addie Mae."

"Sounds like a good place to start."

5 CHAPTER

Aiden pulled up outside the small clinic, parking the SUV in the dirt and rock-filled lot. "Is Doctor Shelton the only physician in town?"

"As far as I know. The hospital is just the next town over. But that could have changed since I've been gone."

They both got out of the car and walked into the one-story building. A bell above the door announced their presence. A brunette in her mid-forties sat behind a desk, typing away at a computer. A name tag clipped to her shirt read, Suzie. She took her time acknowledging their presence, as if she had all the time in the world. "Can I help you?"

Her eyes widened before she plastered a fake smile on her face that didn't reach her eyes. He'd seen that look before. The one that suggested she recognized Amber. Aiden laid a hand on Amber's back. "We're looking for Doctor Shelton."

"Do you have an appointment?" The woman rose from her seat, clasping her hands in front of her.

"No," Aiden answered.

"I'm sorry." The lady looked anything but, replacing the smirk on her lips with a blank look. "The doctor is booked up today."

Aiden and Amber shared a questioning look as they each glanced around the empty waiting room. "Your waiting room is empty."

A flash of defiance crossed Suzie's face before she smoothed it with a smile. She shrugged her petite shoulders, not bothering to provide any other excuse. "Would you like to make an appointment?"

This woman had bitch written all over her face in a don't-fuck-with-me kind of way. Suzie wasn't a mere receptionist, more like a bulldog in a sheep's disguise. They wouldn't be getting a meeting, not here and not today, if ever. "No, I don't think so." Aiden nodded in understanding. "We'll try and catch him later. Thank you for your time."

Ushering Amber out the same way they'd come, Aiden glanced back to find Suzie watching them silently, her expression almost begging them to insist again. Clearly Suzie knew exactly who Amber was, but why in the world would she brush them off? More questions that needed answers.

"Why did we leave? I didn't even get a chance to tell her who I am. He might have made time for us."

Aiden didn't answer until they were back in the SUV. "You didn't see her face when you walked in? She already knows who you are. He wasn't busy. There aren't any cars in the parking lot, and no one is in the waiting room. Did you know her?"

Amber shook her head. "No."

Aiden eased out of the parking lot and slowly drove down the road, backing into a little nook shielding the SUV behind a large clump of trees and giving them an unobstructed view of the clinic's back parking lot.

"What are we doing?"

"Stakeout. I'd bet money that Suzie is informing Doc Shelton that we just stopped by. He'll be heading out soon so that next time we try he won't be in the office."

"Why would he do that?"

"Don't know." Aiden nodded toward the parking lot. "Right on time."

"Maybe he'll lead us right to her."

"Maybe." Although he doubted they'd be that lucky.

She watched as the doctor turned out of the driveway, heading in the opposite direction. Aiden waited, biding his time.

"What are you doing? He's going to get away." A flicker of apprehension crossed Amber's face.

"Patience, we don't want to tip our hand." Aiden's smile grew, while watching the car drive further away. He was giving the doctor a head start. "This town is so small that, even if we do lose him, we'll find him again within ten minutes."

"Not if he leaves town. Did you ever

think of that?" Her voice rose. "Gooo." She gave a sharp point toward the window. "He might be our only shot at finding her."

Aiden rolled out of the hiding spot in time to see the car make a left at the stop sign ahead.

He followed the doctor at a slower pace and watched as Doc Shelton parked his Jag in front of another brick building. The sign on the perfectly manicured lawn in front read, City Hall. Shelton hurried from his car, catching himself as he tripped over his own two feet and casting a worried glance over his shoulder as he disappeared into the building.

What are you hiding? Aiden parked a few rows back sandwiched between two other SUV's and killed the ignition. "We can either go in to find out who he's talking to and blow our cover, or we can stay put and hope he leads us to your grandma. What do you want to do?"

Amber chewed her nails while debating his question. She continued watching the building like a hawk while Aiden waited patiently for her to decide. A smile split her lips as she pointed at the cameras. "How about both? We call Roman and get him to see if he can get into the video feed and we'll wait."

Now she was thinking like a detective. Maybe she was cut out for this type of work. He tipped his head approvingly of her assessment before pulling out his phone and starting to text. Within seconds his phone beeped with an incoming message. "He's going to email me whatever he finds tonight."

"Great," Amber answered. "Let's hope the Doctor leads us straight to Grams."

"You know there's a possibility he doesn't know, but judging by his actions, I'd say he knows something." The need to reassure her overwhelmed him. Aiden reached for her before he realized his action, stopping himself at the last minute. He rested his hand on the back of her seat. Like a damn kid on his first freakin' date. What the hell was wrong with him? "We'll find her."

Fifteen minutes passed before anyone emerged from behind the tinted glass. The doctor and another man dressed in a suit walked out. They spoke for another minute and shook hands before parting ways.

****

Amber tapped her foot nervously against the floorboard as she watched the doctor get into his car and pull out of the parking lot. Her heart leaped in her throat as Aiden followed at a safe distance. She dug her nails into her palms, ignoring the buildings and locals they passed going down Main Street, staying three cars behind. The doctor pulled into the driveway of a two-story house, leaving Aiden to park in the grocery store parking lot across the street. He backed into position, giving them a straight view of the driveway.

"Do you know who lives there?" Aiden asked, nodding toward the house.

"Milly's grandmother, Addie Mae," she whispered, afraid to take her eyes off the doctor as he got out of the car, grabbing his bag and jacket from the passenger seat.

The door jerked open, and an old woman with white tight curls in her hair came barreling outside. It wasn't the sight of the old woman that made Amber's breath hitch. It was the double-barrel shotgun she was pointing at the doctor's chest, stopping him in his tracks.

"Huh," Aiden grunted. "She looks feisty."

Amber nodded. "She's the best shot in town. Rumor has it her daddy was a sniper and taught her to shoot."

"I'll keep that in mind." Aiden grabbed his gun from the backpack and shoved it in his waistband. Reaching back into the bag, he took out some other items and shoved them in his pocket. He opened his door and stepped out, tilting his head across the street. "Let's go find out what all the fuss is about."

Amber chewed her bottom lip and paused with her hand on the door. "But then we won't be able to follow him."

"Watch and learn." Aiden gave her a sly wink before shutting the door.

He took her hand as they crossed the two-lane street, slowing their pace as they approached the doctor's car from behind. He slipped something out of his pocket before tapping the back of the car.

"I guess you aren't so busy after all, are

ya, Doc?" Aiden announced as they strolled up from behind.

The doctor spun around. His dark brown eyes bulged in surprise. "I...I..." He cleared his throat, trying to regain his composure. "I was making house calls."

"It doesn't look like the lady wants your services."

"Want and need are two different things, young man." Contempt flashed in the doctor's eyes before quickly being masked. "Amber? What are you doing here?"

Amber swallowed around the lump in her throat as the doctor nervously looked up and down the road. Was he looking for somewhere to run, or was he worried that he'd be seen?

"I'm looking for my grandmother." She dropped Aiden's hand and stepped forward. "I hear you two got pretty close while I was gone."

Addie Mae jogged down the steps with the gun still pointed at the doctor, took Amber's hand, and then yanked her behind her as if to keep distance between the doc and her. "Amber, honey, go inside."

The doctor held up his hand. "Addie Mae...now you just put the gun down. She came to see me."

Addie Mae cocked the trigger. "I'm not letting you get your filthy hands on that girl like you did my best friend. Now get the hell off my property," she said through gritted teeth.

Amber tried to step around Addie, but the old woman blocked her. "Wait. He might know where she is."

"You heard me, child. Get your rear in the house and take your husband with ya."

"Wait, how did you..."

"Small town, child. Now do as you're told," she answered without looking back. "You too, Doc. You do as you're told and get the hell off my property before I pump some lead into your ass."

"I think she's right." Aiden held up his hands as he stepped around Addie Mae, giving her a wide birth, and took Amber's hand, leading her toward the front door. "Come on, baby. I think she means business." Aiden ushered her up the porch, through the open door, and into the dimly lit room. Dust particles danced in the streams of sunlight, casting a glow on the old wooden floors.

The crack of the shotgun rang out in the air. Aiden and Amber spun in the doorway to find the doctor running back to the street, his barely attached toupee flapping in the wind before he jumped into the safety of his car. He squealed his tires, kicking up dirt and rocks as he skidded in reverse out of the driveway, leaving tire tracks on the asphalt as he gunned the gas.

Addie Mae grumbled beneath her breath as she stomped into the house and shut her door.

"Ma'am, I'm Aiden Monroe." Aiden held out his hand.

Addie Mae shook her head and walked right passed Aiden's outstretched hand, moving to the curtains to pull them closed. "Well, don't just stand there. Help me close these damn curtains."

Amber and Aiden were quick to help her shut up the house. They stood in darkness before Addie Mae flicked on a few lights.

"I thought you were smart getting yourself out of town." She plopped down in her chair and laid the shotgun next to her, within reach. "I guess you aren't so smart after all. Why in the hell did you come back? Your grandma would be spitting-bullets mad if she knew you'd stepped foot in this town."

Amber moved to sit on the couch next to Addie Mae. "Mrs. Addie, you know why I'm here. Aiden and I came to look for her. Do you know where she is or who broke into her house?"

Addie Mae sighed. Her face softened. "Not yet, but if I know your grandmother, she's holed up somewhere waiting for the storm to pass."

"Mrs. Addie, you seem like a wise woman."

Addie Mae smirked. "Compliments won't get you far in this town, sonny."

Aiden grinned. His baby blue eyes sparkled in humor as a dimple creased his cheek. "I only meant that I bet there's not a lot that goes on in this town that gets by you."

Aiden sat down next to Amber and rested his hand on her leg.

Addie Mae arched one of her salt-and-pepper brows. "Yeah, just like I can tell that

Amber and you aren't married."

Aiden's brows dipped, but he let go of Amber's leg and rested his elbows on his knees, leaning forward. "Why do you say that?"

"That ring is about to fall off her finger, and that ain't a real diamond. Just like I can tell that beneath your shirt you're packing heat."

"And that tells you we aren't a couple?"

Addie Mae chuckled. "Nah, son. What gave you away was the way you laid your hand on her knee. If you were a newly married couple, like I hear that you are, you wouldn't have been so far away from her sweet spot."

"Mrs. Addie," Amber choked out as her cheeks warmed.

Aiden gave a little shake of his head. "Okay..." Aiden pressed his lips together in a fine line. "Or maybe I was just brought up with manners."

"Manners would have kept you in that SUV across the street until I finished my conversation with the doctor and ran him out of my yard."

Aiden chuckled and leaned back on the

sofa, resting his arm behind Amber's shoulders. "I like you."

Addie Mae scooted forward. "I've got enough friends." She dismissed Aiden, returning her attention to Amber. "You shouldn't be here. You know they let that boy go."

"Grams told me about Trent before she disappeared," Amber answered, taking Addie's hands. "Do you know where she is?"

"No, dear, I don't know where she is." Addie Mae's face softened as she squeezed Amber's hand back. "But I do know this. My best friend is a strong woman, and if she's in trouble, she knows what she's doing."

Amber's head drooped forward.

"Mrs. Addie. Why did you say you wouldn't let the doctor get his filthy hands on Amber? Are you saying he did something to her grandmother?"

"Yeah. That son of a bitch tried to kill her. He tried to kill her spirit by making her sell the second best thing she loved next to Amber."

"Her house?"

Addie Mae rose and grabbed her

shotgun. "You two need to leave town. Your grandma would be pissed that you're putting yourself in danger looking for her."

Amber stood. She wasn't the little girl running scared any longer. She was a woman, and finding her grandmother was her only priority. "I can't leave."

"You won't leave," Addie Mae corrected her and let out a long sigh. "You were always a stubborn child," Addie Mae walked over to the window and peered behind the curtains. "You're going to get yourself killed, and then your granny is really going to be pissed at ya."

Amber peeled back the curtain, looking outside. "You and I both know if the roles were reversed, she'd come looking for me."

"I know. Damn stubborn woman." Addie Mae winked. "Just like you." She let the curtains fall back into place. "Do you know how my daddy stayed alive as long as he did?"

"He's a good shot?" Aiden guessed.

"Where did you find this guy?" Addie Mae rolled her eyes and took Amber's hand and squeezed. "He was better at hide and seek than anyone else. He didn't advance on his enemies. He laid his own traps and waited for them to come to him for easy pickings. If you make the bait appetizing enough, they'll swoop in like vultures." She winked, walked over to a table and pulled out a drawer. She handed Amber an envelope with her name scribbled on the front. "She said if anything happened to her, I was to give this to you."

Amber took the envelope and ripped the flap open. "She knew I'd come?"

"Of course she did."

Amber's brows dipped as she scanned the document in her hand. Her gaze shot up to meet Addie Mae's. "She put the house in my name." A lump formed in Amber's throat. "Why would she do that?"

"I'm sure she had her reasons. After those two nitwit cousins of yours tried to get her committed, she knew she had to do something."

Amber waved the paper in the air. "Looks like I've found my bait." A slow smile lit her face. "Everyone wants the house."

"That paints a bull's-eye on your back and makes you the new target." Aiden rested his hand on her back. "And let's not forget Trent. He isn't after the house. He's after you."

Addie Mae put her arm over Amber's shoulders and led them to the door. "You need to be careful, child. Make sure you have all your ducks in a row before you let that information get out. I'm not sure how many people your granny told about it."

Amber nodded in understanding. If anyone knew the property deed was signed into her name, there wasn't any telling what would happen. "Has this information been filed at the courthouse?"

Addie Mae grinned. "I've got someone I trust on the inside waiting until I give him the go-ahead to record the certified copy."

Amber walked out onto the porch, but Aiden stopped in front of Addie Mae. "One more question. Do you know who the developers are that want the land?"

She winked at him. "About time you asked a good question." She walked back into the house, grabbed a flyer from the desk, and handed it to him. "Rumor has it that this company is the one sniffing around. I wrote my number on the back of that flyer for Amber." She covered Aiden's hand. "Don't trust anyone. Ya hear me?" She shook her head. "Everything isn't always as cut and dried as it appears."

Aiden rested his other hand over hers. "I've got her back. You can count on that." He waited for Addie Mae to release her hold before waving the flyer in the air. "Thanks for your help."

"Let me know when you need the cavalry. I'm a damn good shot."

6 CHAPTER

Aiden hopped into the SUV before he opened the flyer and read it. Ryder Inc. He handed Amber the flyer and turned on the ignition. "I've never heard of these guys. Have you?"

Amber shook her head. "Nope."

Aiden shrugged as he pulled the GPS tracking monitor out of the backpack and turned it on. Within seconds, a light started blinking on the screen and he laid the monitor on the center console. "We'll get Marshall to dig into the company to see what he can find. It might give us a clue to what the hell is going on." He tapped the screen to make sure it was working. When the street names popped up, he grinned.

"Is that...."

"Doc Shelton's vehicle." Aiden grinned and glanced her way. "Let's go see what he's up to."

****

Two hours later Aiden parked outside the bed and breakfast and killed the ignition. They'd watched the doctor's office as a few patients came and went, and they'd even followed the doctor back to his modest one-story ranch-style house about a mile from where Amber's grandmother lived. He'd left his curtains open as he walked around the house, picking up clothes and starting laundry before he retired in front of the television with a frozen dinner. Following him hadn't turned up any additional clues.

"How about we grab a bite to eat and regroup?" He was helpless to ease the worry or disappointment in her eyes. They both got out, and he linked their fingers and gave a gentle squeeze. "We're one step closer."

The smile she gave him didn't reach her eyes, which made his gut clench. He'd give anything to ease her worry and take away her fear. When they walked into the B&B, they went straight up to their room, bypassing the people who were already eating in the dining room.

Amber pulled out her gun and set it on the dresser. "You know what I don't get."

"What's that?"

"Why the doctor is acting like he's hiding something." Amber placed her fist on her hip. "If they were an item, and she's now missing, wouldn't he be doing everything he could to help find her, hell, even if it's just to save his own hide? He's got to be at the top of the suspect list. Jilted or jealous lover ranks up there with money and revenge."

"The one thing all of these people have in common is they wanted her to sell the property, for whatever reasons. Property that you now own."

Amber plopped down on the bed and fell backward onto it. "That's another thing that doesn't make sense. She didn't want me coming back here, and now, more than ever, she'd want me to stay away with Trent released. Why sign over her property to me knowing I'd have to come back at some point?"

"She must be dead against letting them get their hands on her property." Aiden lay down beside her on the bed. "Now, no matter what any of them try to make her do, she doesn't have the rights anyway. It still doesn't make sense that she'd put you in danger."

Amber turned on her side and rested her head in her palm. "She didn't have the deed recorded, so technically, no one knows I'm the owner. She didn't use that ace in the hole to make them leave her alone. I bet she was saving that as a last resort."

Aiden let out a lengthy breath as he stared at the popcorn ceiling. "True. She's trying to keep you out of the problem...for the time being."

"She's trying to handle it on her own," Amber agreed and lay back down. "Now that sounds just like her. So what's our next move?"

Aiden sat up and ran his hand over his face. "Food first." He gave her a sideways glance before rising from the bed. "I think better on a full stomach."

"I'm not very hungry." Amber leaned up on her elbows.

"You can keep me company." He held out his hand to pull her up. "I know a thing or two about small towns. There's lot to be learned from people watching at the local diners." Aiden shrugged. "And if that doesn't turn up anything, then we'll hit the bar."

Amber took his hand and let him pull her up. "Why the bar?"

Aiden and Amber walked out of the room. "Bartenders are like therapists. They listen to everyone's problems. Besides, you could use a good stiff drink. It might loosen you up." He wiggled his brows.

"I don't need to loosen up, and you aren't getting me drunk. We aren't having sex."

"How did you go from having a stiff drink to having sex?" Aiden bumped her shoulder as they jogged down the stairs. "Get your mind out of the gutter, woman."

Amber chuckled as she pulled the door open. Amber's uncle came barreling inside, almost bumping into them.

"Uncle Stan? What are you doing here?" Amber asked.

Stan stood momentarily stunned. His gaze swept past them and Aiden turned to see what held Stan's interest. Milly stood behind them. Her cheeks were flaming red.

"I just came to pick up the sweet potato pie Milly made for me." Stan cleared his throat. "Her pie is the best in three counties." Stan glanced down at his hands, fiddling with his keys. "Where are you two headed?"

"The diner, to see if we can find some clues about Amber's grandmother."

Stan stepped around them. "Good luck. I've already been asking, and no one knows anything."

"Maybe we'll get lucky," Aiden answered and led Amber, by the elbow, out of the B&B.

Amber glanced over her shoulder toward the closed door as Aiden led her to the truck. "Did that seem weird to you?"

"She must make some amazing pies,"

Aiden answered, not wanting to tell Amber what he really thought. Milly's blush and Stan's fidgeting with his keys told Aiden that there was probably something a bit more than pie orders going on. Milly was into older men and Stan was robbing the cradle.

Amber tapped her foot nervously against the SUV floorboard as he drove to the diner. When she started chewing her nails, he pulled her hand to his lips and kissed her palm. Apprehension radiated from her in waves.

"Relax."

Amber's cheeks turned pink as she slipped her fingers free. "Sorry. It's just been a long time since I've seen the people in this town. There's no telling what rumors started after I left."

He pulled into the diner, parked the SUV, and looked up into the large windows covering the front. "They look busy."

"It's one of the few places to eat in town," she answered as they got out. Aiden entwined their fingers and gave a gentle squeeze.

"Are you ready?"

She nodded and inhaled a long deep breath. "Yep, it's time to face my past."

The bell above the door dinged and all eyes turned in their direction. Aiden rested his hand on Amber's lower back and moved closer to her side as she glanced around the establishment until everyone in the quiet room resumed talking. Families and couples occupied most of the tables. The mayor and sheriff sat next to each other at the counter sipping coffee with the two detectives that had interviewed Amber. Detectives Lawson and Sims gave them a curt nod in passing. The sheriff's jaw clenched and the mayor's eyes widened. Yeah, they could learn a lot from watching expressions alone. Several eyes watched as Aiden guided Amber to an empty table near the wall where he slid in across from her so he could keep eyes on all of the occupants.

"I'd say they still remember you."

Amber pressed her lips together and clasped her hands. "Yep." She glanced over her shoulder once more before turning around.

"Care to wager who's the first to approach us?"

"The waitress," she guessed.

"Uh uh...not counting the staff." Aiden glanced around her. "I mean which diner do you think it will be?" He smiled. "You have the advantage. I only know the ones sitting at the counter."

She glanced over her shoulder once more before slowly turning back. She licked her lips. "My guess is Danny. The guy in the red flannel shirt."

Aiden located the man with brown hair wearing a red plaid shirt looking their way. A blonde sat next to him bouncing a toddler on her lap. "Why him?"

"We were friends."

"I don't think so." The waitress interrupted them to take their orders before he continued. "He's with the blonde who's wearing a wedding ring, and considering the baby on her lap looks just like him, I'd lay money that is his family. My guess is on the detectives, specifically Lawson."

"Why?"

Aiden's grin grew. "Because he's headed our way, and considering the bathrooms aren't in this direction, it can only mean one thing."

The waitress returned with their drinks before Lawson stepped forward. "Ms. Cantrell, Mr. Monroe." Lawson pulled an empty chair over and sat at the end of the booth. "I hear you two have been busy."

"Mr. Lawson." Amber clasped her hands together. "We've all got the same goal. Do you have any new leads on my grandmother?"

He shook his head. "I can't discuss our ongoing investigation, Ms. Cantrell."

"Amber, please," she corrected him.

"Amber, you two shouldn't have come here."

"Where else would we be? Her grandmother is missing, and we're going to find her," Aiden said, resting his hand on the back of the booth.

"Are you trying to stir up trouble?" Lawson cocked his head and narrowed his eyes in Aiden's direction. "From what I hear, you've already approached Doc Shelton, and let me save you some trouble. He doesn't know anything. We've already interrogated him."

Doc Shelton's actions contradicted that

statement, but that wasn't what piqued Aiden's interest. A smile slid on Aiden's face. "How do you know we've been to see him? I can count on one hand the number of people who knew that information."

Lawson's mouth parted before he snapped it closed and cleared his throat. "Small town."

Aiden's brow rose. "That's the best ya got? Small town?"

Lawson rose and returned the chair to the other table. He rested his hands on the table and narrowed his eyes. "There's a lot more going on here than either of you realize. So stay out of my investigation. I'd hate to have to lock you up for interfering."

"How's that going to look for you?" Aiden slid out of his seat and stood eye to eye with the investigator. "Arresting the distraught granddaughter of the missing woman, a woman who came back to a town she left that couldn't protect her from a damn stalker, just to look for her grandmother." Aiden shook his head. "No, I don't think so, Detective. Not unless you want every media outlet on God's green earth to converge on this town, not to mention the security specialists I work with. They could show up and start poking around." Aiden crossed his arms over his chest. "It's your call, Detective. I just hope you can stomach the consequences, because I can guarantee there will be consequences the likes of which you've never seen."

Lawson's brow rose and he nodded. "Just friends, huh?" He shook his head. "Yeah, I don't think so. Maybe I should arrest you both for interfering in our investigation."

Aiden pulled out his phone and typed on the keyboard before he hit send. "Go ahead. I have the troops on standby." Aiden stepped forward. "Grams might not have had anyone to help when she went missing, but I can assure you, that's not the case with either of us."

Amber slid out of her seat and stepped between Aiden and the jackass. She rested her palm over Aiden's heart as it threatened to beat from his chest. Adrenaline coursed through his veins as he balled his fist. "Aiden."

She rested her other palm on his cheek,

and he lowered his eyes to meet hers. Her cheeks held a red tint, her eyes glassy with tears. "Let's not do this. I'm sure Detective Lawson is doing his best."

Aiden's thumping heart slowed as he ran his thumb over Amber's lip. He'd morphed into protection mode like that of a lion protecting his pride. Amber turned to face Lawson, and Aiden rested his palms on her waist and pulled her back against his chest.

"Lawson." The sheriff's deep voice carried across the quiet room. He tilted his head toward the door.

Aiden and Amber watched as Lawson followed orders and left with the sheriff before they retook their seats. "Well, that was interesting."

Amber rubbed her temples, her face pinched as if she had a migraine.

"Well, look what the cat dragged in," a tall brunette women announced as she and another woman approached the table.

Amber spun in her seat and let out a sigh of resignation as the girls motioned for Amber and Aiden to scoot over. The woman who slid in next to Aiden held out her hand.

"I'm Maria, Amber's cousin, and this is Bree." She gestured across the table.

"It's a pleasure." Aiden shook her hand.

"No, honey, the pleasure's all mine. Welcome to the family." Maria grinned as she flipped her long hair over her shoulder. She smiled and winked at Aiden before turning to face Amber. "I heard you got hitched, but Daddy didn't tell us you landed a hunk."

Maria placed her hand on Aiden's knee beneath the table and started to slowly move it up his thigh.

He swiped it off his leg, and Maria giggled, gave him a sideways glance and batted her eyes. She moved her hands on top of the table and linked her fingers together. "Just checking to see if you're faithful, darlin'."

"I worship the ground my wife walks on. No other woman could tempt me, especially when it took me years to convince her to marry me," Aiden announced. "But then again, I'm sure you'd never know that type of devotion." He leaned in. "Hitting on another woman's husband is frowned upon where we're from."

Amber released a pent-up sigh and leaned forward, pegging Maria with a glare. "Maria, keep your hands off my man, or I'll break every bone in your hands. Are we clear?"

"Ugh," Maria grunted in disgust. "Like you could."

"Try me," Amber growled.

"So you're the cousin that tried to get Grams committed so you could sell her property. I bet it really chaps your ass that you didn't get what you wanted."

Maria's smile fell and her face hardened. "I always get what I want."

"Not at this table, honey." Aiden's grin grew.

"Maria," Bree choked out from the other side of the table. "Quit being a bitch." A hint of pink colored Bree's cheeks.

"I can tell when I'm not wanted." Maria slid out of the seat and stormed off across the diner to sit at another table.

"You can say that again," Amber mumbled.

"If I'd known she was going to act like that, I would have never brought her over here."

"You aren't your sister's keeper." Amber patted Bree's arm. "God knows no one can control her."

Bree hesitated before speaking, as if trying to find the right words. "I just wanted to know if you've found anything yet. Daddy told us you were going to look for Grams."

"Not yet," Aiden answered. "Do you know where they all looked?"

The waitress interrupted their conversation, delivering their food before Bree could answer.

"Yeah, I was part of the search party. The police sent up a helicopter and searched the mountains while the rest of the search party searched on foot. I think they sent a couple boats out on the lake with radar and searched that too."

"So you expect foul play?"

Bree pressed her lips together and glanced over her shoulder before she leaned in and whispered, "Personally, I thought Trent kidnapped her to get you to come back to town. When they released him from prison, he came back and tried to get Maria and me to tell him where you were. He said he needed to talk to you, and when we told him we didn't know where you were, he looked angry. He called us liars and said that he knew you were still in contact with us. He said he had proof."

"What proof?"

Bree shrugged. "He didn't say. He just said he was going to Grams' house. We called and warned her. I just hope we weren't too late."

Aiden exchanged a worried look with Amber before asking, "Did you tell the investigators?"

She nodded and pulled out her phone. She hit a few buttons and turned the phone to Aiden flashing him a picture before showing it to Amber. It was a profile shot of a dark haired man with a goatee. His lips pressed in a fine line as he walked out the café door.

"Is that Trent?" Aiden asked.

Amber took the phone, her eyes widened in fright. "When did you take this?" Amber asked.

"I took the picture here at the café, before I called to warn Grams."

"And you showed this picture to the

detectives?"

"Yes."

"When?" Amber asked still looking down at the phone. Her face turned pale.

"Three days ago. The day after we found her house trashed."

7 CHAPTER

After finishing their meal, Amber climbed into the SUV and clicked her seat belt in place while waiting for Aiden to get in behind the wheel.

"Bree is either lying or the investigator is a good actor."

Aiden started the ignition. "You caught that too?"

"Yeah, when I told them about my conversation with Grams about Trent, they looked surprised, but if what Bree is saying is true, then they already knew."

Aiden pulled out onto the road and headed back toward the B&B. "If we're going to entertain the idea that Bree is telling the truth, then what possible proof could Trent have had that he knew you were in contact with them. I mean think about it. If he had proof, he would have known where you were."

"Might explain the notes I've been getting." She shook her head. "But even if he had someone else leaving them for me, surely the delivery boy would have told him my location after he got out of prison." Amber shook her head. "I'm not buying it. Something doesn't add up."

"Yeah," Aiden whispered. "You can say that again."

Aiden parked in front of the B&B and killed the ignition.

"I thought we were going to the bar."

"It's been a long day. We'll hit that place tomorrow night if we can't find her. I need to make a few phone calls."

"Okay." They both got out of the SUV and headed for the porch.

"I'll be up in a minute. I'm going to make the calls out here. I haven't had time to sweep the room for bugs yet."

She gave an uncertain nod but walked

inside, leaving him on the porch. Aiden pulled out his cell and sat down in one of the rocking chairs.

"Speak," Marshall answered.

"We haven't found her yet, but I need you to have one of the guys check into something for me."

"What's that?"

"Long story short, we've been told Trent showed up here and claimed to have proof that the family knew where to find Amber."

"How is that possible? He was in prison."

"I know. That's what I'm having trouble wrapping my head around. If he did have proof of that, then it means someone was feeding him information, regardless of whether they told him her exact address. I need someone to look into whatever visitors Trent had or see if you can get a phone log or anything that might tell us who he had contact with."

"Consider it done," Marshall grunted. "Do you think he's involved?"

"I don't know," Aiden answered as he stood and paced into the parking lot. "I also need a background check on that investigator who came to see Amber. He threatened to throw her in jail for interfering in the investigation and implied there was more going on than meets the eye. Either he lied to us about knowing Trent was released, or her cousin is lying about Trent showing up saying he had proof and she told the cops. Either way, we need to know whatever you can dig up," Aiden leaned against the warm hood of the SUV. "Something is wrong here. I just haven't pinpointed what it is."

"You mean something other than her missing grandmother?"

"Yeah. I think you might need to send Roman. We need answers, and the only way we're going to get them is if we dig deeper than I can do when sticking by Amber's side. I'm limited to the type of recon I can do while watching her back."

"You got it. What else?"

Aiden turned and leaned against the SUV. "I need a full workup on the town doctor and his receptionist. If there is any dirt, maybe we can use it to get him to tell us the truth."

"Let me talk to him," Sophie called out

in the background.

"Honey, just a minute. I'm not done," Marshall argued.

Sophie's voice grew louder. "Let me have the damn phone, Marshall."

"Those damn pregnancy hormones," Marshall grumbled.

"I hope you enjoy the couch tonight, dear," Sophie said in a sing-song voice before she changed her tune and spoke into the receiver. "Aiden, how is she?"

"She's worried, but everything will be okay."

"Aiden, tell me the truth....now."

"Her cousin is a bitch; her uncle almost shot me, and the doctor is hiding something, but we haven't seen Trent."

"That's more like it. Okay, now I need you to do something for me."

"Sophie, he's doing everything he can," Marshall grumbled in the background.

"Anything for you, Soph. What?"

"Don't leave her side. Someone is going to die."

"How do you know that?" Aiden paused in his pacing.

"How do you think I know?" Her voice

rose an octave. "I'm being told, but the spirits won't tell me who."

"Shit." Aiden rushed up the porch stairs into the B&B and bumped into Uncle Stan leaving. "Hang on, Soph," Aiden said before pressing the phone to his chest.

"Are you back for another pie?" Aiden asked. "Or are you just leaving?"

Stan's jaw ticked. "Where's Amber? Does she know you're on the phone with another girl?"

Aiden smiled. "As a matter of fact she does. Now what's your excuse?"

"None of your damn business." Stan brushed by Aiden, knocking his shoulder as he passed.

Aiden put the phone back up to his ear. "Sorry, on my way up to the room to check on Amber; I ran into her uncle."

"At the B&B?"

"Yeah, he apparently likes the pie."

"It's a little late for pie," she said.

"Depends on what type of pie," Marshall teased in the background, making Sophie giggle.

"We have to go. I'll have that stuff checked and have answers as soon as possible," Marshall said before the line went dead.

Aiden jogged up the stairs to the third floor to find the door left ajar. He pulled the gun from his waistband and toed the door open with his boot. "Amber?" He cautiously stepped inside, checking behind the door before he closed it. The balcony door stood open, the curtain blowing on the incoming breeze. The sound of the shower running made him pause. He tightened his grip on the gun as he moved through the room, stepping into the closet with his gun clutched against his chest. He flicked on the light and released a pent-up breath. The water from the shower was the only muffled noise in the room.

Aiden quietly turned the knob and pushed the door open as the water turned off. Amber slung the shower curtain open. Her mouth parted and her eyes widened. Aiden held his finger to his lips with the gun still up in the air as he backed out and closed the door behind him. He hurried back across the room and killed the light before moving through the dark room to the balcony. He peered, pressing his back to the drywall, glancing out onto the balcony before stepping out and twisting to check the other side. The balcony was empty.

Amber stepped out next to him in her robe, a gun in her hand, her wet hair clinging to the fabric. "There." She pointed at a dark figure running in the distance. The man stopped and glanced back as a motion sensor from the nearest house clicked on. Amber's breath hitched. "Son of a bitch."

"Trent?" Aiden asked as he pointed his gun in that direction.

"Yep." Amber lifted her gun and took aim right as Trent ran into the shadows of the wooded property behind the house.

Aiden pulled Amber back inside, shutting and locking the balcony door. He tugged the curtains closed and locked the door before he let out a breath he hadn't realized he'd been holding. "Was the window open when you came in?"

"No," she answered, glancing around the room.

"He must have been in here." Aiden moved her away from the door to sit in one of the chairs away from the window. "Did you leave the door open behind you?"

She shook her head. "No."

"That means Trent either had a key or he could have already been inside hiding when you came in. It's possible he waited for you to get in the shower so he could make a run for it."

"There's only one problem with that theory." She stood, unlocked the balcony door and walked outside with him following. She looked over the railing. "How in the hell did he get down if he went out this way?"

Aiden pointed to a trellis that ran next to the storm drain. "There. That's how I would have done it." He pulled Amber inside again and locked the door.

"He had me. He could have easily ambushed and killed me while I was naked in the shower." Amber shivered before rubbing her arms. "Why didn't he?"

Aiden moved slowly around the room, cataloging their stuff. "It doesn't look like anything is missing or out of place." He gestured with his head. "Check your suitcase."

Amber unzipped her suitcase and rummaged through her things. "Nothing is gone. Not that I can tell."

Aiden unzipped his suitcase and lifted the lid. "Son of a bitch."

"What?" Amber asked, moving to stand next to him. "What's missing?"

"Our files." Aiden dropped the top.

"What would he want with those?" She plopped down on the bed. Her robe opened, giving him another glimpse of her creamy skin, which he'd had the opportunity to see when she was naked in the shower. Aiden squatted in front of her and closed the gap.

"It's hard to form a coherent thought when you're half-naked. Why don't you put on some clothes?" He cleared his throat, his hand on her bare thigh as he held her gaze. He'd expected to see anger and confusion staring back at him, not the heat in her eyes, the lust that called to him, begging him to make a move. Her vulnerability lay wide open. He cleared his throat again. "Please."

"You're the first guy to ever ask me to put them on and not take them off." She chuckled and stood, dropping her robe from her body. Uninhibited, she moved to the suitcase and pulled out a pair of boy shorts and a tank top and slid them on. She held out her arms. "Better?"

"For the record..." He closed the distance between them, resting his hands on her waist. His fingers toyed beneath the hem of her tank top, touching her warm skin. "When we sleep together, I won't ask you take your clothes off. I'll do it myself." He kissed her neck and scraped his teeth against her skin. "With my teeth."

Aiden winked as he stepped back, releasing her. Goosebumps appeared on her arms. Yeah, she had that look, almost ripe for the picking, but this wasn't the time or the place. He turned and moved back to his suitcase.

"I'm not sure why he'd want the files," Aiden admitted. "There isn't anything in them that will tell him where to find you. Your history, which Roman pulled didn't contain your current address, only your past before you moved."

Aiden zeroed in on Amber nervously twisting her fingers together. "Amber, where's your ring?"

"I..." She turned toward the dresser

where her necklace lay. "I left it right there."

A smile split Aiden's lips. "Finally."

"What?" she asked, dropping to her knees to look beneath the dresser.

"We caught a break. That ring has a tracker in it. We'll let him get settled tonight, and in the morning, we'll know exactly where he is."

Aiden grabbed some clothes out of his suitcase. "I'm going to take a shower. Try and get some sleep."

"You expect me to sleep knowing he's out there."

Aiden tossed the clothes on the bed and sauntered up to her. "Does my wife need me to take her mind off of things?" He pressed a kiss to her neck. "I'd be more than happy to oblige." He pulled her closer and let her feel just how happy he was.

"Sex?" She rolled her eyes, yet her body gravitated toward him. "I told you; you aren't the right guy for me. Have you forgotten?"

"Your mouth is saying one thing, but your body is telling me another." He ran his hands beneath the tank top to her back, his fingers splayed across her back.

Her voice turned sultry. "Aiden, you aren't making this easy."

His lips twitched. "Aren't I?" He pulled her closer, and she licked her lips. He watched the movement with a heated expression, imagining tasting her again, kissing her not because of their cover, but because she wanted to. He could read the hesitation in her eyes, the war she was having in her mind.

"You're right. I promised to be a gentleman, and I'm failing miserably." He dropped his hold and stepped back, unable to look away. Ready to face his own disappointment. "I'm going to take a shower."

She waited until he turned to close the door. "Aiden..."

"Yeah."

"You're not failing."

He nodded and closed the door, giving her space, willing to take matters into his own hands to undo the effects of seeing her naked in the shower with water dripping off her luscious body. It wouldn't be the first time, and after sleeping in a bed with her, it probably wouldn't be the last.

8 CHAPTER

Aiden lay still beneath the covers. Amber's palm rested above his heart, and her legs lay tangled with his. The rise and fall of her chest pressed into his side. Her warm breaths heated his skin, and he was afraid to move. He savored the feel of her in his arms. A smile split his lips, while he thought of all the ways he could wake her up: a kiss here, a nibble there, a game of poke. He closed his eyes remembering the precise minute she'd rolled into his side and snuggled in her sleep. He'd pulled her closer and stayed true to his word. He'd stroked himself to completion in the shower to thoughts of her naked body. His reprieve was short-lived when he climbed in bed intent on keeping distance between their bodies. Within the hour, she'd snugged up against him, and no matter how honorable his intentions had been, he couldn't stop himself from enjoying the feel of her in his arms.

Her breast pressed into his side, her tiny tank top and boy shorts the only clothes keeping him from feeling her smooth, warm skin. He'd fallen asleep some time during the night, waking up when she'd tossed her leg over his and moaned in her dream. Aiden glanced at the clock on the bedside table, debating what time he'd wake her up and how much torture he could endure without his baser needs getting the best of him. He closed his eyes, and a vision of her naked body from the shower last night filled his mind again for the millionth time. His eyes shot open again.

"Go back to sleep." Amber's groggy voice broke the silence in the room.

"I'm afraid that's not possible," Aiden answered, rubbing lazy circles on her bare arms.

Amber let out a sleepy sigh and opened her eyes to look at him. "Why?"

Aiden licked his lips and glanced up at the safety of the popcorn ceiling. He began searching for the dot he'd left off counting in the middle of the night to help him forget her proximity. "Because I'm fighting the urge to flip you over and settle between your sweet thighs."

He glanced down at her face to find her looking up at him. He could see the questioning look on her face, the wheels turning in her mind.

"Relax. I'm a big boy, and this isn't prom night. I can control my urges." He kissed her forehead and moved to slide out from beneath the covers.

"Aiden." She rested her hand on his arm, stilling him from getting up. "I'm sorry you're stuck with me."

He returned to his pillow and turned to face her, resting his hand on her arm. "Amber, when have you ever known me to do something I don't want to do?" His gaze softened. "I'm not stuck with you. I'm here because I chose to be. Marshall and Sophie might have ordered me, but the truth is, they couldn't have stopped me from coming with you."

Her brows dipped at his confession. Her mouth parted, and he held his breath for her response. When she pressed her lips together, he realized what she'd been trying to tell him. She didn't want this. She honestly didn't want him. His heart and gut clenched.

He pulled his mask back into place, his head back in the game, and winked at her. "Now get that sexy ass of yours dressed, and let's go catch our ring thief and find your grandmother."

He slid off the bed and headed for the sanctuary of the bathroom. He clasped the sink and lowered his head, letting out a resigned breath.

"Aiden," Amber called from the other side of the door.

"Yeah." He pulled it open, and she rushed inside. Clasping his face in her palms, she pressed her lips to his in a kiss that had nothing to do with their cover. She pressed her warm curves to his. Her rapid heartbeat thumped wildly against his chest as she leaned against his body. She parted her lips, and their tongues dueled for control. His fingers slipped up into her hair, and he tilted his head to deepen the kiss. Damn if he didn't want to take her up against the bathroom door, on top of the sink, or to carry her back to the bed and strip her bare.

Goosebumps covered her creamy skin as she reached between their bodies and cupped his hard shaft. He broke the kiss with a moan, resting his forehead against hers. "Amber." She slid her hand up his shaft, and he covered her palm with his, stilling her actions. "Stop."

"Tell me you don't want this."

Aiden clenched his eyes closed, fighting against the urge to take her. When he reopened them, he found her eyes clouded with desire and lust. "You know I do, but you're not thinking clearly." He cleared his throat. "You said it yourself. You're looking for a husband, and I'm not that guy. I could spend hours worshiping your body, leaving us both fully sated, but you'll regret it."

"I've made a lot of mistakes in my life, but this isn't one of them." She slipped her fingers free and slid them beneath his boxers. She circled his shaft and ran her thumb over the head, eliciting a moan from deep in his chest. His palms rested on her waist, and he inched them beneath the fabric and slowly up her sides to cup her breasts as he kicked the bathroom door closed and backed her against the wood.

"You sure about this," he asked in a ragged breath against her lips.

"Less talk, more action." She cupped his balls in response.

"Your wish is my command." A smile curved his lips as he squeezed her breast and lowered his head, using his teeth to slide the tank top strap down her arm to give him better access to the creamy flesh hidden beneath. Kissing a path above the hem, he used his teeth to pull the hem farther down for easier access to her mounds. He sucked a creamy globe into his mouth, scraping his teeth against her skin as he fondled the other breast. She moaned, making his cock grow harder in anticipation as he slowly took over control to give her what she demanded. He tweaked her other nipple between his fingers, and then he heard knocking. He groaned and clenched his eyes closed, ready to kill their visitor. "Someone has rotten timing."

"Can't we just ignore them," she whispered. "Maybe they'll go away."

The knocking turned into pounding, and Aiden righted her shirt and stepped away. "Wait here. I'll get rid of them."

She nodded.

He stepped out of the bathroom. "Just a minute," he called out and slipped into a pair of jeans, ready to throttle whoever was making all that noise.

Aiden unlocked the door to find Roman impatiently waiting. "What took you so long?"

Aiden stepped back, letting Roman into the room. "We had a long night and just woke up."

Roman paused, giving Aiden a sideways glance. "Has something changed?"

Talk about a loaded question. Was Roman referring to their investigation or to whatever the hell was happening between Amber and Aiden? He decided to answer the obvious. "Someone snuck in the room last night while Amber was in the shower."

Roman grunted. "Where were you?"

"Downstairs on the phone, talking to Marshall."

"Where is she?" Roman asked, glancing around the room. "She isn't hurt, is she?"

"I'm fine," Amber answered, walking out of the bathroom in the clothes she'd worn to bed.

Aiden noticed Roman's reaction to seeing Amber half-dressed. His blank expression did little to hide the heat in his eyes. The son of a bitch was interested. She walked over to the suitcase, grabbed some clothes and slid them on.

Aiden smacked Roman's shoulder. "She's off-limits."

He jerked his gaze back to Aiden. "To who?"

"Uh, boys, I'm still in the room." Amber smiled and shook her head. She walked over to Roman and kissed his cheek. "I didn't know you were coming."

"Looks like I might be too late." Roman gave her a rare smile before glancing at Aiden. "So what did your intruder take?"

Aiden grabbed a shirt from his bag and

finished getting dressed. "Her tracker ring and our files."

"Any idea who the dumbass is?"

"We saw Trent running off last night."

Roman's brows dipped. "He's crawled out from under his rock?"

"Looks that way," she answered, walking over to the window and opening the curtains. "We're going to track the ring and find him today."

"I guess I was wrong. Looks like I didn't miss all the fun." Roman picked up Amber's gun from the dresser and popped the clip, checking to see if it was loaded before shoving it back into the ankle strap and handing it to her.

When they were ready to leave, Roman took point, and Aiden brought up the rear, and what a fine rear he was watching. Amber glanced over her shoulder. A sexy smile played on her lips.

****

Amber watched as the blip appeared on the screen when Aiden pulled up the tracking signature on the ring. When the streets popped up and a blinking light flashed the location, her breath hitched as dread filled her bones. She stared at the GPS, unable to find her voice.

"What's wrong? Do you know who lives here?" Aiden rested his palm on her arm.

She nodded, unable to believe her eyes. "That's my Uncle Stan's address. This must be a mistake."

"I'm not so sure about that." Aiden put the SUV in gear and pulled out. "I saw him leaving out the front door last night."

"I'm sure there's a perfectly good explanation," she whispered to reassure herself, returning to watch the passing greenery out the window. "There has to be."

They rode in silence the ten miles to her uncle's property which sat between her grandmother's and Doc Shelton's house, in a ten mile radius down the country road. Her uncle's beat-up pickup was parked in the driveway. Aiden parked and turned off the ignition.

"Maybe I should go up alone." She glanced at Aiden. "He could be armed, and he'd never hurt me."

"Like hell," Aiden answered and tossed his door open.

"Yeah, not a good call, Amber. Like you said, he could be armed," Roman echoed. "We know he at least has the ring. It's not like we're shooting in the dark."

Amber and Roman got out of the SUV, and Aiden knocked on the door. He waited and knocked again. No answer.

"You think he's home?" Roman asked, moving across the porch to the windows, which were covered by curtains that blocked their view.

"His truck is in the driveway," Amber answered and walked back to the door. "Uncle Stan, it's Amber. Let me in," she called out.

No answer.

"He doesn't ever lock his door," Amber said, turning the doorknob and pushing the door open, letting the sunlight stream in. Uncle Stan's unmoving body lay in the middle of the floor. She gasped, hurrying into the room. Aiden grabbed her, pulling her back against his chest.

Aiden handed her to Roman. Placing his finger to his lips, he drew his gun. He pointed to the door, and before Amber could protest, Roman had whisked her outside. He drew his own weapon and scanned the horizon as she pressed her back to the bricks. Her hands trembled as she reached for her gun. Minutes ticked by that seemed like hours before Aiden walked out.

"It's clear." He moved to Amber and shoved the ring on her finger. "He left it out in plain sight on the kitchen table."

"Is he..."

She knew Aiden's answer without him having to tell her. Sorrow filled his eyes, and her heart clenched. "You're mistaken." She shook her head. "He can't be dead."

"I'm sorry, Amber," Aiden whispered and tried to pull her into his arms. She brushed him off and sidestepped him, hurrying through the front door to her uncle's lifeless body. Blood covered his shirt and the hardwood floors beneath his body. She reached for him.

"Don't touch anything." Aiden touched her arm. "You'll contaminate any evidence."

A gasp and crash from the doorway had them spinning and lifting their guns toward the door. Milly stood at the doorway. Her hand covered her mouth. A pie plate lay shattered at her feet, the pie ruined. Her gaze stuck on the sight of Uncle Stan's body as tears trickled down her cheeks.

Amber ushered her out of the house and eased her into a porch swing. She could hear the guys inside as they talked in hushed tones. Aiden and Roman each carried on separate conversations on their phones as they stepped outside and into the driveway.

The tears turned into sobs as Milly covered her face with her hands, and Amber knelt down in front of her. She looked up, swiping her tears. "Is he dead?"

Amber swallowed around the lump in her throat. "Yeah."

Milly bolted upright, almost knocking Amber over. "No...no... This isn't right." More tears streamed down her face. "He promised me he'd change." Her head dropped, and her shoulders shook as she rubbed her belly. "He promised us. He'd be a good daddy." Milly dropped to her knees. Her whole body shook as she sobbed.

Amber went to her and hugged her.

Milly clutched her, her tears soaking Amber's shirt. Aiden and Roman stood behind them, silently watching.

"Milly, I'm so sorry," Amber whispered and rubbed her friend's back. "We'll find who did this. I promise."

Minutes passed before Milly leaned out of the embrace and swiped her tears again. Amber moved her to sit back on the swing.

Aiden squatted in front of her and took her hands. "Milly, why was Stan at the B&B so late?"

She sniffled. "He was there to see me. I told him about the baby a week ago, and he didn't take the news too well. He was there trying to reassure me that everything was going to be fine. Insisting he'd changed his ways, that he'd be a better man for the baby and me. He said he had one more thing to take care of before we could get married and settle down." More tears flowed and she covered her face with her hands. "Oh God."

"Did he tell you what he needed to do?"

She looked up and shook her head. "No." She visibly swallowed. "I figured he was still worried about his mom." Her eyes pleaded for Amber to understand. "He was still looking for her, just like you."

"Did he have any enemies? Anyone that would want to see him hurt?" Roman asked.

Milly rubbed her lips together. "He owed five grand to a loan shark, but he'd paid him off."

"Did he say where he got that kind of money?" Aiden asked.

Amber could see the uncertainty in her eyes. She was holding back. Amber took Milly's hands. "Please tell us, Milly."

Amber met Aiden's worried look as the moments ticked by.

"He overheard a conversation between Doc Shelton and the mayor."

"Was he blackmailing one or both of them?" Roman asked.

"I don't know." Milly closed her eyes and gave a gentle shake of her head. "The only thing he told me was that he overheard them saying that they had someone on the inside that could make the land deal go through. They had a way of dealing with the hold-outs."

"Did he say who?"

"No." Milly met Amber's gaze as sirens in the distance wailed louder as they got closer. "Amber, he was worried about your grandmother. You have to believe that. He had his faults, but he was a good man." A tear slipped free. "I loved him." She glanced over at the window. "And now he's gone." She rubbed her belly. Her head dropped on her shoulders. "My baby is never going to know his father."

9 CHAPTER

Amber clutched Milly's shoulders, offering silent support as they all watched the gurney carrying Uncle Stan's body being wheeled by. Amber didn't have any time to grieve for the man who had saved her life, not when there was another life hanging in the balance. Fear clogged Amber's throat. A killer was now officially running free and on the loose in her town. Amber's idea that her grandmother's disappearance was nothing more than an impromptu trip, to get out of town to avoid the land investors, was slowly tearing at the seams. Her uncle's death was a heartbreaking reminder that the town she'd grown up in was as corrupt as any other. The mayor and doctor were neck deep in this shit, and Amber had every intention on finding out just how far their plans went.

Several grueling hours later, Amber had given her statement and offered her alibi at the police station, along with everyone else who had been onsite when the sheriff and his men had finally arrived. Now Aiden, Roman, and Amber sat in a booth at the diner in quiet conversation as they tossed ideas back and forth on the best way to proceed. Amber's mind was somewhere entirely different, still trying to rationalize that her Uncle Stan had died.

The bell above the door chimed, pulling her attention in that direction. Maria's angry glare met Amber's. Her eyes narrowed, and her nostrils flared. Bree tried her best to hold her back, talking in hushed tones through clenched teeth. Maria brushed her off and stormed over to the table.

"This is all your fault," she seethed through gritted teeth. "He's dead because of you. Why couldn't you just stay gone? No one missed you."

The room quieted as the diners curiously looked their way.

"This isn't her fault," Aiden protested. "Amber didn't have anything to do with it. She's just here looking for her grandmother since she's the only one concerned that the woman is missing."

Amber laid a hand on Aiden's arm. "Don't."

"They can't just come in here and accuse you of something you didn't do," he argued.

"They lost their dad, and I lost my uncle," Amber whispered and slid out of the booth. "When we got there, he was already dead." She reached for Maria to hug her and Maria smacked Amber's hands away.

"You killed him," she screamed.

"No, she didn't," Bree said, pulling Maria back. "The cops don't know who killed him yet, but I'm sure it wasn't Amber." Bree turned Maria to look at her. "She's our cousin. She'd never hurt Dad."

Maria's eyes narrowed on her sister. "Bree, she's not the innocent little girl that we grew up with. She's not fooling me."

Maria crossed her arms. "You don't believe me? Just ask your boyfriend. He'll tell you the same thing."

Maria stormed off and out of the diner. Bree gave Amber an apologetic look. "I'm sorry," she whispered before running after her sister.

Amber watched through the window as the two sisters argued outside. They gestured wildly with their hands before they took the argument out of sight.

"Who's her boyfriend?" Aiden asked.

Amber shrugged as she slid into the booth. "I have no idea."

"Don't you find it odd that Maria is convinced Bree's boyfriend agrees with her, and this is the first time we're hearing about the guy?"

"Nothing in this town makes sense." Amber's throat clogged, as she fought back the tears gathering in her eyes. The anger and fear had finally caught up with her. Her heart clenched, dying a little more as her world crumbled around her. "If you'll excuse me, I'm going to the restroom."

Amber walked into the bathroom and let out a breath. She moved to the sink and doused her face with cold water in an attempt to wake herself up from this never-ending nightmare. The door behind her opened and closed, yet she didn't care. The water hid her tears. A hand appeared in front of her, dangling a paper towel within reach. Amber met Suzie's reflection in the mirror.

"Great." Amber tossed her arms up in the air. "What do you want? Are you looking for more juicy information to run back and tell the Doctor?"

"No, now dry the tears. I don't have much time," she said in whispered tone.

Amber took the towel. "What do you want?"

"To give you this." She held out an envelope. When Amber didn't reach for it, Suzie grabbed Amber's hand and closed her hand over it. "If you want to know where she is, meet me by the old oak tree in the park. You know the one."

"What?" Amber tried to open her hand, but Suzie squeezed it harder. Something in the envelope poked into her palm.

"The one where Trent and you had your picnic."

"How did you...."

"Never mind that. I don't have time to explain. Tonight at midnight. Come alone or don't come at all. At the first sight of those guys at your table or the cops, I'll leave. Do you understand?"

"What's to stop me from calling the cops right now? I'll have you arrested before you make it back to work."

"I doubt that." Suzie rolled her eyes and removed her hold on Amber's hand. "I know what happened to your grandmother." She gestured to the envelope. "And soon, you will too." Suzie hurried to the door and pulled it open. "But only if you're alone. You can't tell a soul, or she's as good as dead."

"Suzie, please, just tell me where she is."

Suzie pressed her lips together and gestured to the envelope. "That tells you enough that you can trust me."

Suzie disappeared out of the bathroom, and Amber slid her finger beneath the flap of the envelope and tipped it over. The necklace and cross her grandmother always wore slid out into her palm, and Amber's legs grew weak. The ball in her belly felt like concrete. She unfolded the note inside, quickly scanning the contents. Her grandmother's handwriting stared back at her like a beacon in the storm. Amber's heart started beating again.

Amber,

You shouldn't have come looking for me. You're in danger now too. I can't tell you much through my letter, but you can trust Suzie, and to prove that this is me and that I'm okay, you can tell Sophie that she won't be seeing me anytime soon.

I love you. Stay safe, my sweet child.

XOXO,

Grams

Tears clouded Amber's eyes. No one in town knew about Sophie's abilities, except Grams. She was safe. Amber clutched the letter to her chest and let out a sigh of relief as the renewed tears slipped down her face.

"Amber, you okay in there?" Aiden asked from behind the closed door.

"Yeah. I'll be out in just a minute," she answered and then hurried to stuff the letter back in the envelope and shoved it into her pocket. She latched the necklace around her neck and clutched the cross. She doused more water on her face and patted away the evidence of her tears before she yanked the door open to find Aiden leaning against the wall waiting for her.

"I thought you fell in." He grinned.

Amber smiled back, probably the first genuine smile she'd given him since the plane touched down yesterday afternoon. "I'm surprised you didn't break the door down to rescue me," she teased.

"I thought about it," he answered and tossed his arm over her shoulder. "How about we blow this joint?"

"That's the best idea I've heard yet." Amber scanned the diner as they made their way to the door. "Where's Roman?"

Aiden didn't answer until they were outside. "He went back to the B&B to get a room and look over the files that Marshall emailed him."

"What files?" she asked as she slipped into the SUV.

"Last night I asked him to pull backgrounds on Doc Shelton and his receptionist."

Her mouth parted as Aiden started the SUV. "Did they find anything?"

"Don't know yet. That's what Roman went to go look at. He's also going to look into your uncle's financials to see if he can trace the money back to either the doctor or the mayor. If we're going to nail everyone involved, we're going to need proof."

She gave a slow nod. "So what's next? Who are we going to talk to?"

Aiden tossed the SUV into gear, but he didn't drive. "Right now, we're going to lay low until we get more intel. With your uncle's death, I'm afraid no one is going to talk to us." He closed the distance between them and cupped her cheek. "I'm sorry about your uncle." He pressed his lips to hers in an easy kiss.

"Me too." The highs and the lows of the day had her strung tight one minute and ready to fall on her ass the next. "I feel so bad for Milly and her baby, not to mention my Grams when she finds out. Losing another child is going to kill her."

"I'm sorry, baby. Since we've got a little while until we hear from Roman, how about we do something out of the norm?"

"I know just the thing." Her eyes lit up with excitement. As much as Amber hated to admit that they were at a standstill, she was a bit more relaxed about not looking now that she had some semblance of proof that Grams was okay. Seeing her in person would have been better, but hopefully, tonight she'd know exactly where to find her. Amber clutched the cross hanging around her neck. "How about I show you my favorite place in the whole world?"

Aiden grinned and reached for her hand, threading their fingers together. "Point the way."

10 CHAPTER

Aiden parked outside of Grams' house and killed the ignition.

"Come on. It's about two miles back on Grams' property. Are you up for a hike?" Amber asked as she got out.

"Sure." Aiden grinned and laced their fingers together, and he let her lead him down a well-used path. "I bet you were queen of these woods growing up."

"Curious is more like it." She smiled. "Growing up, I liked to explore. I wasn't a typical girly girl. I was more of a tomboy at heart."

Aiden chuckled as they veered off and

stepped over a log. "I bet all the boys liked you."

She shrugged. "Nope. They liked Bree and Maria. They didn't look at me the same way."

"I can't believe that."

"It's true," she protested and led him farther into the forest.

He glanced around at all of the huge trees. The overhead sunlight was hidden by their tall branches. "This is the perfect setting for a serial killer to pop out."

"You aren't scared, are you?"

"Of course not." He pulled her closer. "I'll save you and shoot his ass."

"My hero," she teased and held her hand to her heart.

"You don't strike me as the type of girl who needs a hero," Aiden joked and bumped her shoulder.

"I like to think I can take care of myself."

"You know, it wouldn't kill you to rely on someone else to take care of you every once in a while."

She gave him a sideways glance but didn't respond. They trekked the rest of the way while engaged in an easy banter that didn't include any relationship talk. He asked about her dreams and ambitions and teased her about having to work with Jack. She teased him back about his playboy ways and how she was ruining any chance of his hooking up with a local by pretending they were married. They pushed through the last bit of brush, and he stopped dead in his tracks. Steam floated up from the blue water as birds chirped on nearby trees.

"You have a hot spring?"

She nodded. Her smile grew by the second. "Yep, not many people know about it since it's on my grandma's land. Whenever I wanted to escape, I'd come here."

Aiden unlaced his boots, took off his socks, and dipped his toes into the warm water. "Wanna skinny dip?" he asked over his shoulder.

"I'm way ahead of you," she answered and walked by bare-ass naked. His mouth parted as he watched her slowly and seductively sink into the water, covering her breasts from his sight.

Aiden flicked the button on his jeans, lowered his zipper, and stepped out of his clothes. His cock grew in size the longer her hungry gaze stared at him. "How many boys did you bring here?"

A hint of pink touched her cheeks as she turned her head and floated to the other side of the hole. "You're the first."

Aiden walked into the water, straight over to her, and pulled her back against his chest. He kissed up her neck, and she tilted her head to give him better access. "I'm honored."

He held her stomach so she couldn't float away. His hard cock rested against her ass. She rested her hand on his and slowly moved it down her body.

He nibbled her ear, and his other hand squeezed her breast, slowly rolling her nipple between his fingers. She moaned, and her head rested against his shoulder.

"Are you in a hurry?" he whispered into her ear.

"If I was in a hurry, there would be a lot less talking and a lot more making waves." She smiled and turned her head to capture his lips. Her hot mouth melded with his. Their tongues dueled as he slipped his fingers through her folds and swallowed her moan. His pressed a finger inside her slick channel, and she turned in his arms, wrapping her legs around his waist and moving her body against his hand. His thumb circled her clit, and he watched with a hungry gaze as her head fell back and her eyes slipped closed. He quickened the pace of his fingers, adding another finger to her tight channel, and watched as she neared her orgasm. Her legs tightened around his waist as she climaxed. She moaned in ecstasy as her channel contracted and tightened around him. He didn't pull his fingers free until she came down from her high, easing them out of her as she pressed a hot and heated kiss to his lips.

His straining body pressed tightly against hers as she broke the kiss. Her labored breathing and the rise and fall of her chest began to slow as she rested her forehead against his. "I needed that."

"I was happy to oblige," he whispered and pressed another kiss to her lips.

She raised her body, positioning her entrance over his cock and covered the tip.

"This isn't about me. This is about you."

"Is that so?" she asked and tried to

move his hand.

"Yeah, and I'm afraid the condom is in my wallet and probably not effective in water."

She stilled and moved her hand to his shoulder. "Rest assured, I'm covered."

He tilted his hips, entering her tight channel. "Thank heaven for unanswered prayers."

He moaned as he seated himself fully inside of her, holding her still as she acclimated to his girth. "You're tight."

"It's been awhile," She blushed as she answered.

"Me too," he admitted. "Let me help you remember how good it feels." He eased her up his shaft and then back down. She met him thrust for thrust as their lips entwined. Her fingernails scored a path down his back as he tried to hold out long enough to give her another orgasm. He held on to her hips, pumping his shaft in and out of her tight channel as it tightened around him. She kissed his neck, sliding her teeth over his skin, and he hardened even more. She held his gaze, looking deep into his soul as he quickened the pace. The move was so intimate between them that unspoken words got stuck in his throat.

She radiated perfection in an imperfect world. His heart clenched with renewed awareness that this might be the only time they had together. He brushed that thought out of his mind as his orgasm built. Her channel tightened around him. He felt her tremors and could tell by the little sounds she made, and the way her eyes slid closed, that she was close.

"Look at me," he whispered.

Amber's eyes slid open. Her erratic heartbeat matched his as he filled her and pushed her over the edge. Her channel tightened around him, milking him of his essence, taking him with her.

They stayed like that long after they both found their release, staring into each other's eyes, and he wondered if she was thinking the same thing as him. Did she want more? Did she feel what they had in that moment, when it was just the two of them? He did. Did she?

Aiden swallowed around his dry throat as he stared into her eyes. For the first time in his adult life, humor escaped him as his heart clenched. He was unable to read her expression, her mind. He had no idea what she was thinking, and that thought terrified him. "Say something."

"I..."

Rain pelted their heads, and she glanced up at the trees with a wide smile. "It's raining." She laughed and held her arms out to the side. "Come on. I know the perfect place."

She slid off of him, and they both hurried to get dressed. She took his hand and pulled him through the forest.

"I think it's going to be hard to top the hot springs."

She flashed him a wide smile. "Nothing will top the hot springs," she answered, pulling him into the cover of a nearby cave.

He glanced down into the darkness. "How do you know this place isn't home to a hibernating bear?"

She shrugged. "I don't, but I can tell you I've never seen one here, and I've played in these caves for a long time."

He moved to stand behind her, wrapped his arms around her waist, and kissed her neck. "I never would have guessed any of this was back here."

"Oh, there's more," she said excitedly. "The caves run from here to a rundown factory on the property too. When the old textile mill went under on the plot of land behind Grams, she bought that property too. Let's just say she hates having neighbors. Growing up, my friends and I were busted playing hide and seek in the building. Grams warned us about playing there. She was afraid we'd fall through one of the rotting boards and break our necks."

"I wonder if they searched that area for her."

"I don't know." Amber turned in his arms and pressed her lips to his. "Aiden, I have something to tell you."

Voices carried through the tunnel as lights from a flashlight flickered off the walls.

"Shit," he whispered as he grabbed her hand and ran with her to the nearest thicket of trees.

They crouched behind the brush; he pulled out his gun and she had hers. What seemed like an eternity passed, though it was mere minutes before two men stepped out of the opening. The taller of the two was bald. His arms were covered in tattoos and he wore a thick gold chain around his neck. He spoke with a New York accent. The other man was dressed in a suit, minus the jacket. He was shorter.

"These damn mosquitoes are going to piss me off."

"I told you that you should have used bug spray," Baldy answered.

"I can't believe he brought us to the sticks. We should be in New York at the club surrounded by beautiful women."

Amber pulled out her cell phone, turned the phone on silent, and turned off the flash. She waited for the other one to speak before she snapped a few pictures.

"Penance for screwing up the hit," Baldy answered. "Once we find that old broad and finish what that little prick started, we can be on the first plane outta here," he grumbled as they trampled through the forest in the opposite direction.

"I hear her other granddaughter is in town. She came just like *he* said she would."

"I'd like to get me some of Maria."

This thug knows Maria?

The short one smacked Baldy. "Not that one, you idiot, the other one."

Aiden slowly maneuvered Amber and himself around the bush, staying out of the assholes' sights. Minutes ticked by as they waited for the two to get farther away, Aiden constantly checking over his shoulder toward the cave to make sure no more men were coming.

"We've got to go. There could be others and they have more firepower than us," he whispered.

Amber nodded, shoved her cell in her pocket, grabbed his hand, and hurried him through the forest, knowing it like the back of her hand. They made it out in half the time it had taken them to get to the hot spring.

Each gasping for breath, they hurried into the SUV. Aiden didn't waste time throwing the vehicle into reverse and getting Amber somewhere safe, somewhere where they had more firepower and extra muscle.

11 CHAPTER

Aiden shut the door to their room and threw the locks. He pulled the curtains closed and checked the lock on the balcony door. The sun had started to dip behind the horizon. He paced the length of the room. His brows dipped as a frown marred his face. "Shit."

Amber slid her wet clothes off and grabbed another shirt and pair of jeans. "It's not as bad as it seems. We've got the upper hand. We might not know who they are, but we know where to find them."

She walked into the bathroom, grabbed a brush and ran it through her hair. "We'll send the picture to Marshall. He'll do his thing, and then we'll know what we're dealing with."

"How can you be so calm?" he asked and moved back to the curtain.

"Because we know they didn't succeed in killing my grandmother. You heard them; they mentioned a botched job, and the fact they knew Maria's name, tells us enough." She walked over to him and placed her palms on his arms. "I know every inch of those woods. Once we know who we're dealing with, we'll figure out why they're here and how they play into all of this."

He nodded. "Intel first, storm the compound later."

She lifted on her tiptoes and pressed a kiss to his lips. "Can it wait until we order room service, Rambo? I'm famished."

"I guess." Aiden rolled his eyes. "If you insist on turning all girly on me."

She chuckled and patted his chest, walking over to the B&B phone and dialing downstairs. "An hour ago, you didn't mind me being a girl."

Aiden wiggled his brows. "No...no...I didn't mind at all."

A knock sounded on the door, and Aiden checked the peephole before he answered. Roman walked in with a laptop under his arm.

"Just in time, I'm ordering room service."

"Good idea. After what I found, you won't be leaving this room again," Roman grumbled.

Amber raised a brow at his remark. "Keep dreaming." She turned her attention to the phone and placed a huge order for the three of them. Her plan to sneak out at midnight was becoming more complicated by the minute. She tried to keep the worry from her face as Aiden explained what had happened during their afternoon tryst, keeping the things that happened between them to himself. She hadn't missed the worried look that passed between Aiden and Roman as she sent the pictures to each of them and another message to Marshall to see if he could work his magic and figure out the identity of the pair of goons in her forest.

"Well, I looked into the doctor's background, and his receptionist, and I have to tell you that things aren't looking so hot for the doctor. I'm still waiting for the information on Trent."

Aiden plopped down on the bed, resting his back against the headboard and lacing his fingers behind his head while Amber slowly paced the room.

"We had to dig deep on the doc. They found the typical information. Where he went to school, a bit about his background, but not much else, so Marshall made a call to one of his FBI contacts. It turns out that Doc Shelton was already on their radar, even before he moved into town. It appears he's being investigated because of the obscene amount of prescriptions he's writing and unethical insurance billing practices."

"Elaborate." Aiden sat forward.

"Take Grams for instance."

Amber paused in her tracks and met Roman's gaze.

"He prescribed pain killers in her name, and someone else tried to get it filled."

Roman crossed his arms over his chest. "When the insurance company had a question about the billing code and appointment, they'd called her instead of his office." Roman rested his hand on Amber's arm. "She must have figured out what he was doing because your grandmother called the FBI to report him."

"Why didn't she tell me?" Amber sat on the edge of the bed.

"That's probably why she broke things off." Aiden reached for her hand and gave it a gentle squeeze.

She slipped her hand free and held both hands up. "Okay, assuming that my uncle was blackmailing the doc and the mayor, then that means the mayor is in on whatever is going down."

"That might be the reason Addie Mae told us not to trust anyone," Aiden reminded her.

"The thugs in the woods are part of the plot to obtain the land, and seeing them in my caves and hearing them mention the attack on Grams," Amber spun to face Aiden, "all sounds drug related."

Aiden stood, walked to the window, and

peered behind the curtains. "You're forgetting one important fact." He glanced over his shoulder. "Trent."

"He was in prison," Roman reminded them. "Maybe he got in with the wrong crowd and wanted to expand his resume."

"Maybe," Amber whispered as a knock sounded on the door. Roman had his gun pulled and held behind his back, as did Aiden as he peeked outside. "It's room service."

A young woman pushed a food cart with covered trays into the room. A pink hue covered her cheeks as she took in the occupants and hurried to leave without waiting for a tip.

Aiden started loading up a plate, filling it full of fries and a hamburger and handed it to her before making his own.

"What did you find on the receptionist?" Amber asked as she sat down at the small table. She popped a fry into her mouth.

"I've scoured the Internet and our contacts. Suzie Mayfield does not exist. At least, not the one who works for the doctor."

Amber swallowed down her fry and sipped her drink. "How can she not exist?"

"I hacked into the realtor's database and pulled up the contract she signed to rent her apartment and used the information she supplied to see what I could dig up on her. Every single phone number, for the references she used, has been disconnected. Her last known address is a vacant lot in New York." Roman shrugged. "I'm still looking, but so far, every lead has been a dead end."

"Did you check the property owner of the vacant lot?"

Roman's brow rose. "Of course. It's listed under a shell company, and I'm still trying to untangle that trail. As of now, that woman is a ghost."

Amber swallowed around the bite of her burger and swiped the napkin over her lips before abandoning her plate.

"Well, that ghost is the only person who knows where my grandmother is." She walked over to her discarded jeans, slid the envelope out of the pocket, and handed it to Aiden before retaking her seat. "She cornered me in the bathroom at the diner and gave me that."

Aiden's brows dipped as he read the note from Amber's grandmother. He handed the paper to Roman and met Amber's gaze. "How come you didn't tell me?"

"She told me to meet her in the park tonight at midnight and to come alone." The atmosphere in the room turned thick with apprehension.

"You aren't going." Aiden stood and crossed his arms over his chest. "It's a trap."

Amber laced her fingers in her lap. "Trap or not, that is my grandmother's writing, and no one in this town knows about Sophie's gifts. I know for a fact my grandmother would never put me in harm's way. That was her little code that everything is okay."

"I have to agree with Aiden." Roman folded the note and placed it on the dresser. "There's too much we don't know. Especially about Suzie."

Amber stood and took a deep, calming breath. "That woman is the only lead to finding my grandmother. If you think for one minute I'm just going to let her slip through my fingers, then you two have another thing coming. I am going to meet her in the park."

"Then we're going with you." Aiden crossed his arms over his chest and pegged her with a challenging glare.

"Not happening." Amber shook her head. "She said to come alone, or my grandmother is as good as dead."

"And if you go alone, then you're as good as dead," Aiden countered and closed the distance between them. "I promised Sophie I wouldn't let anything happen to you, and I intend on keeping that promise, even if it means tying you to the bed."

Amber raised her brow. "Just try and stop me."

Roman held up his hands. "Time out. Everyone needs to take a breather."

Amber spun on her heels and moved across the room to retake her seat at the table. There wasn't a chance in hell she'd let them talk her out of her plan.

"Aiden. I'm armed." She held up her left hand. "I have a tracker, and you guys will know how to find me if I don't come back."

"She has a point." Roman's face

softened.

"And on top of that, I have proof that she knows where my grandmother is. This isn't some wild goose chase where I'm going in half-cocked. This is a credible lead." She stood and closed the distance between them. "I can do this." When he didn't reply, she continued. "I *am* doing this."

The fine lines on his face deepened as he sidestepped her and left the room. Any hope that he would understand went out the door with him.

"He'll come around. It's the right tactical move, and he knows it."

"Then why is he being so stubborn?"

Roman's lips twitched. "I think you know the answer to that, even if he doesn't."

"You don't think..."

"I don't think, Amber. I know."

"Aiden is just a friend. Granted, that status changed to friends with benefits, but that's all it is. That's all he's capable of. He told me that himself. If I was Sophie, he would be acting the same way."

"That's where you're wrong." Roman grabbed his plate and moved to the table.

"If you were Sophie, he'd let you track your lead because it's the right tactical move to make."

"He just doesn't trust that I can take care of myself."

"There's a difference between trusting you to take care of yourself and worrying that something might happen to you."

"And you know this how? Because you're an authority on the subject?"

Roman's jaw ticked, and a flicker of sadness crossed his eyes. "I've worked with Aiden long enough to tell when he's in love." Roman tilted his head. "And I think you might feel the same way."

"You're crazy," Amber argued and moved to the curtain to peer down below at Aiden as he paced the parking lot with a phone pressed to his ear. Her heartbeat sped at the crazy suggestion, but she shook her head. "He doesn't love me. He's not capable."

****

Hours later, Amber dressed in black as Aiden checked the ammo in her gun. "You get out of there at the first sign of trouble."

Amber took the spare gun with the ankle holster and strapped it on. "Aiden, we've been over this."

He handed her the gun for her waistband. "If she attacks, you shoot to kill."

"I'm not killing the only woman who knows where my grandmother is." Amber rolled her eyes and attached the second holster to her jeans.

Aiden's jaw ticked and set into a fine line. "Amber, I'm serious."

"I am too," Amber placed her hand on his arm. "If anything happens, I'll shoot her in the knee. She's not walking away without giving me answers."

Aiden cupped Amber's face between his palms. His green eyes softened as he searched her eyes. "Whatever you do, don't lose that ring."

Amber smiled and pulled her grandmother's necklace, with the ring attached, out from beneath her shirt. "I won't."

"Are you sure I can't talk you out of this?"

"Aiden." Amber dropped her gaze, tired of arguing about how stupid he thought she was being.

He lifted her chin with the crook of his finger. "I don't want to lose you."

Her lips tilted at the corners. "Sophie won't blame you. She knows I'm stubborn."

"This has nothing to do with Sophie. I don't want to lose you. Understand?"

She wasn't having this conversation. She didn't have time to guess what he meant by his words. She stepped out of his hold and crossed the room to grab her phone. "Don't worry. I'll be back before you know it."

Aiden was behind her, his hands on her hips as he turned her to face him. She could see the uncertainty in his eyes and feel the tension in the room. She pulled his head down to hers and pressed a kiss to his lips. "Don't go getting soft on me."

Aiden chuckled. "I've never been accused of being soft."

Amber winked. "I might test that theory later." She sidestepped to the door, pulled it open, and then paused to look at him. "Thank you for coming to town with me to search for my grandmother."

Aiden nodded, his lips pressed into a worried line as she shut the door, leaving him behind.

12 CHAPTER

Amber clung to the shadows as she trekked through the back entrance of the park toward the shining light posts in the distance, just past the oak tree where they were to meet. Her pace slowed as she neared. She was still trying to piece together the one part of the puzzle that didn't make sense. How Suzie knew about the tree.

"I didn't think you'd come," a male voice said from behind her. The one voice she'd spent years trying to forget.

Her fingers trembled at the sound.

Amber spun around and whipped out her gun, pointing it at the dark figure as he stepped out from the shadow of the tree. Trent stilled, his gaze fixed on the gun.

"Where is my grandmother?" Amber asked through gritted teeth while flicking the safety off her gun.

"She's safe," Trent answered and made a move to stick his hands in his pockets.

"Keep your hands where I can see them."

Trent stilled and raised his hands. "You've changed."

"And you haven't." She narrowed her eyes, watching him like a hawk. With each step he took, she countered, keeping the distance between them. "You're still taking people against their will. You must have enjoyed prison because I'll see to it that you go back."

"No...I'm not going back."

Amber braced herself for Trent's outrage and anger. And yet, it never came. He held an air of calm and confidence as he studied her. "Prison changed me. It forced me to grow up, and I have you to thank for that."

"Is that why you took my grandmother?"

"I didn't take her. I saved her," he answered and stepped closer.

"Not another step." She cocked the trigger.

"If you don't believe me, you can ask her yourself." His lips tilted up in a smile as he gestured to his pocket. "I have her on speed dial, but I need my phone."

Amber nodded, leveling him in the gun's sights. "One wrong move and you aren't walking out of here."

His lips twitched as he looked past her. She felt the metal barrel in her back. "I could say the same to you. Are you okay?" Suzie asked him.

"Yeah," he answered as Suzie pushed Amber's gun to aim at the ground, surprising Amber when she didn't try and take the gun away.

"We aren't here to hurt you." Suzie lowered her weapon as Trent hit a button on his phone and held it out for Amber to take.

"Hello, hello." She heard her grandmother's voice.

"Grams," Amber answered on a breath, never dropping Trent's gaze. "Where are you?"

"I'm safe, child. Trent saved me."

Amber shook her head. "How?"

"He came back to town looking for you, to apologize, and thank God he did."

Amber turned her back to Trent and paced away into the trees. "Tell me where you are and I'll come get you."

"Sweetie, I'm safe, and that's all you need to know right now. Suzie will explain the rest."

"Grams..."

"Amber, baby. You need to burn the deed change. You're in danger now." Amber heard men's voices in the background. "Baby, I need to go. We'll talk again soon. Just get out of town. Okay?"

"No." Amber's voice rose. "I'm not leaving without you."

"Amber, we'll talk again soon. I promise, but I've got to go. I've been on the line too long."

There was a click in the line followed by silence.

"Grams."

"Sorry, but she was instructed to keep it short." Suzie walked over, took the phone, and tossed it to Trent. Suzie pulled out a badge and flashed it to Amber. "My name isn't Suzie Mayfield. I'm FBI Special Agent Suzie Mason, and I'm working undercover to bring down a drug trafficking ring of huge proportions."

"I don't understand." Amber glanced between the two. "How are you involved?"

"I'll give you a few minutes to explain while I check the perimeter, but then we need to go."

Trent nodded. "As luck would have it, my cellmate, Vinny Scarpello, was a drug runner for the Santini mob, and not only that, he liked to run off at the mouth. At night, he was the worst, keeping me up all hours talking about how the Santinis were in the process of setting up a new shop and he got busted with drugs while scouting the area. When he made the mistake of mentioning Polk, I started paying more attention, learning everything I could. I had every intention of coming back to find you, so I could tell you how sorry I was, but I needed to make this right too."

He stepped closer to her, and she stood her ground. "I really am sorry."

She pushed his apologizes to the back of her mind. "That doesn't explain about my grandmother."

"I went to the diner for coffee when I got back to town. I was looking for the right words that might convince your grandmother to call you, even if I couldn't see you face to face." Trent held Amber's gaze. "In the booth behind me, I overheard a conversation about how some old bitch wouldn't sell her property and the town doc had failed in trying to convince her. I heard them joking about how they were going to scare her into selling, and if that didn't work, they were going to kill her."

"How did you know they meant my grandmother?"

"Your cousin and that cop sat down with them." Trent let out a deep breath. "So I pulled my baseball hat down to cover my face and left as fast as I could without trying to draw attention to myself."

Amber crossed her arms over her chest. There was one problem with Trent's story. "My grandmother would have never left with you."

"Oh, you're right about that." Trent leaned against the oak tree, propping his foot up. "She had company when I showed up. Suzie was already there, and thank God she was. She believed me when I told her Vinny was my cell mate. It wasn't until I told them about your cousin sitting in the booth that your Gram believed me too."

"Maria's always looking for trouble. Grams wouldn't have been surprised."

Trent righted himself. "Amber, it *wasn't* Maria in the diner that day. It was Bree and that detective, Jim Lawson."

Amber's heart fell into her stomach. His words felt like a punch to the gut; the air left her lungs. Lawson and Bree?

"She believed me then. She knew they were dating. She said she caught them on the property snooping around."

"Ten minutes later, I placed your grandmother and Trent under police protection," Suzie said, appearing out of nowhere. "Trent is our star witness, and your grandmother, well, we were worried for her safety."

"That's why she took her robe."

Suzie grinned. "She said she never leaves home without it."

Amber nodded, the haze of the events surrounding her grandmother's disappearance clearing into focus. "And here I thought Bree was blackmailing the mayor and the doctor like my uncle had."

"What?" Suzie asked.

Amber explained what they'd uncovered while searching for Grams. "I would have never guessed Bree was involved."

"Love makes you do crazy things," Trent added.

She snapped her gaze to him at his words.

"I am sorry."

"You made up for it." Amber started pacing the clearing and pulled out her phone. She shot off a text to Aiden, letting him know she was fine and ended it with a code word that only the two of them would understand. Hot springs.

Within seconds, the phone vibrated. *We have a visual on you.*

It figured, Aiden had gone against her wishes, but she didn't have time to deal with him now. Her mind was busy racing with how to handle her cousin and get her grandmother's life back to normal.

An idea flashed in her mind, and she spun around. "I know where they're setting up shop and exactly what to do." She nodded and pulled out her phone. "Give me your number and I'll text you the plans."

Suzie rattled off her cell number and Amber saved it. "Keep my grandmother safe and I'll be in touch." Amber started a light jog into the trees.

"Wait, what are you going to do?"

She slowed and turned. "Strike a match and watch the fireworks." She grinned. "Try not to get burned in the process," Suzie called after her.

13 CHAPTER

Amber wasn't surprised when Aiden and Roman jumped down from the trees as she made her way back to the B&B.

"Did you guys hear all that?" she asked.

"Yep, sounds like Lawson and your cousin are in on everything."

Amber nodded as Aiden linked their hands together. She lifted them and looked up at him. He gave her a sexy grin but remained silent.

"It's time to up the ante and take away their reason for being in my town." She nodded, a plan slowly forming in her head.

Roman gave her a sideways glance. "What did you have in mind?"

She grinned. "You know, my Grams always told me that old building was a hazard. I think it's time to burn that bitch down to its foundation."

"Destroy any potential operations." Aiden squeezed her hand. "That's going to make you more of a target."

"I'm counting on it, but we have to leave the B&B and find another place to stay. I don't want Milly or the baby getting hurt."

"Agreed," Aiden said, and Roman grunted.

"We need reinforcements if we're going to come out of this unscathed." Roman slipped out his phone and started texting.

"We need to figure out who has their hands in the cookie jar, and I know exactly how to do it."

Roman returned to his room to start the ball rolling on getting more people into town. Aiden and Amber went back to their room and closed the door, locking it behind them. He swung Amber into his arms. He held her tightly as he kissed her. His fingers reached for the hem of her shirt and yanked it off before her hands went for the button of his jeans.

"You're lucky nothing happened to you," he whispered between kisses. "I would have had to tear this town apart."

Her breath came out in pants as he rushed through relieving her of clothes before lifting her into his arms and carrying her to bed. He settled between her thighs and held her gaze. "I seem to recall you accusing me of being soft."

Amber wound her arms around Aiden's neck. "Yeah. You ready to prove me wrong?"

"Oh yeah." He kissed her and winked before sliding home and reminding her that he was anything but soft.

****

They spent the next two days waiting for the others to show up and doing some recon on the abandoned building that wasn't so abandoned anymore. Marshall and he had to call in several favors and IOU's to be allowed to participate within the FBI's operation. The armed thugs stood guard as delivery trucks came and went from the property. When Marshall supplied them with a map showing the heat signatures on the property, she didn't ask where the information came from; she was just happy that it had come. They were all staying at her grandmother's house now. The two-story building was cramped with Aiden, Roman, the other team of men and her. Even with the crowded accommodations, they made it work, using shifts to patrol the property and keep a lookout. Amber had called Addie Mae the next day to have her contact, at the courthouse on standby, file the papers. She'd arranged the day and time when she'd arrive. They all realized that their anonymity was coming to a close when the first thug showed up and was met by a wall of men carrying far more firepower than what the thug had in his possession.

When D-day came, Amber texted Suzie, letting her know the plans. Roman and the guys were going to converge on the building while Amber decided to take her claim public.

"Are you sure you don't want me to go with you?" Aiden asked as he walked her to the SUV.

"You need to stay and coordinate the takedown with the feds. You need to be here." She ran her hands up his chest. "Besides I'll be fine. Suzie is meeting me at town hall."

Aiden handed her a pen. "Remember, if you turn the cap right for a green light, you can use it as a normal pen. Turn it left for death. Even though the blade is small, it's laced with enough poison to stun your attackers and let you get away."

The pen had been ingenious. A little spy gadget the guys had come up with so that she could get into the courthouse undetected, but she wouldn't be completely unarmed while inside the walls.

He cupped her cheek and gave her a slow, leisurely kiss. "Be safe."

Amber pulled out the necklace with the cross and her tracker ring. "I always am."

She spotted Aiden in the rearview mirror watching her until she was out of sight. She gripped the wheel tightly as nerves racked through her body the closer she got to town.

Amber parked in front of the courthouse and gauged the cars in the lot. She spotted the FBI van before getting out of the car. Suzie shut the door and met her with a nod as they approached the steps of the building.

"How's my grandmother?"

Suzie nodded toward the van. "She's with an agent and Trent in the van. We sent the other agents to help your guys with the raid. Are you ready for this?"

"More than ready." Amber nodded, and they walked up the courthouse stairs.

Suzie flashed her badge before stepping through the metal detector, and Amber's heart raced as she emptied her pockets, leaving the pen, along with her keys, in the basket before she cleared the detector without so much as a beep. They sent her items through the x-ray machine, and she held her breath until her things popped out the other side, the makeshift pen going undetected.

They followed the room numbers to the Register of Deeds Office and stepped inside. Addie Mae's friend behind the desk smiled and ushered her over. "I've been waiting on you."

"We appreciate this."

"Did you bring your ID?"

Amber nodded and pulled it out of her pocket, keeping the pen clutched in her hand.

The woman made a copy of the ID and passed it back to her. "If you'll just sign at the tab."

Amber scribbled her name, thankful she turned the cap the correct way.

Suzie led her toward the rear of the building. "The van was supposed to pull around back so you could see your grandmother for a minute."

"Thank you," Amber slipped the pen into her back pocket and hurried to follow along. They pushed out the back door and Amber's heart raced in her chest. She was anxious to see her grandmother.

14 CHAPTER

Aiden checked his gun one last time as he and the others gathered around the floor plan of the warehouse lying on the dining room table; a final chance to make sure everyone knew the plans. Roman's phone beeped, and his brows dipped as he read the message.

"Fuck me," he whispered and met Aiden's gaze.

"What?"

"Marshall got the visitor logs on Trent, and you're never going to guess who stopped by," Roman said through gritted teeth and then hurried to the laptop, logging into his email.

Aiden's mouth parted. His heart stopped beating as a picture filled the screen of Bree and Lawson signing in.

"Oh, this isn't good." Aiden whipped out his phone and fired off a text to Amber. When she didn't reply, he knew she was in trouble. "Text Suzie. This was a fucking setup," he yelled as he grabbed Roman's keys, banged out the door, and jumped off the porch.

"What about the warehouse?" Roman called out.

"Take it down. Those sons of bitches aren't getting her property," Aiden growled. "And that shithead isn't getting her."

"What if you can't find her? You're going to need the team to help."

Aiden clenched the keys in his hands. "We're married. I'll track her."

Roman nodded. "Good luck."

"You too."

****

Suzie pulled her weapon and pointed it at Trent, who stood just outside the back door, in front of the van, with the barrel of a gun pressed against Grams' temple. The other federal agent, tasked with watching Grams in the van, lay unmoving and bleeding at Trent's feet.

"Let her go," Suzie demanded.

Trent's eyes narrowed on Amber. "This was never about her land or the fucking drugs."

Amber raised her hands. "You're right." She nodded. "This was about you and me. You left those notes...but how? You were in jail."

Trent's lips twisted at the corners. "Your cousin is craftier than you give her credit for."

If Amber got out of this alive, she was going to kill her cousin. "Please...let Grams go. Take me instead."

Trent's nostrils flared.

"You can't do this." Suzie tried to grab Amber to stop her from moving closer to Trent. "He'll kill you."

Amber glanced over her shoulder. "I have to."

She held up her hands and moved closer to Trent. "Now let her go."

Trent grabbed Amber and held the gun to her head, shoving Grams at Suzie. He pointed the gun at her grandmother and pulled the trigger. Grams collapsed to the ground as blood gushed from the wound on her leg.

"You bastard." Amber struggled to get free and Trent held her tighter with the gun shoved up against her head.

"It's a flesh wound. Don't be stupid," he whispered in her ear as he backed up into the van, pulling her with him. "Shut the door."

Amber met the fear in her grandmother's eyes and watched as the blood drained from her face. Suzie was beside her, the gun still trained on the van door, as Amber slowly slid the door closed.

Trent flicked the locked and shoved her to the driver's seat. "Drive."

She hurried to obey while Trent had the gun pressed in her ribs. "Where are we going?"

Trent's nostrils flared again, uncertainty in his eyes.

"Don't tell me you haven't thought this far ahead."

"Shut up," he growled in her ear while surrounding the driver's seat from behind. He shoved the gun harder into her side. His other palm landed on her breast and slid beneath her top. "I've thought about this every day since they locked me up. First, I'm going to fuck you, and then I'm going to kill you. Unlucky for you, your fucking uncle isn't here to stop me this time." His fingers dug painfully into her breast and she whimpered.

"That's just a taste of what I'm going to do to you." He leaned forward and bit into her neck." She screamed and used her fingers to scratch at his face. The van swerved onto the easement. The bumpy gravel had Trent releasing her and grabbing to get a foothold. Tears welled up in her eyes as her shoulder throbbed in pain. She needed to get out of the driver's seat if she was going to get away from this bastard. She was a sitting duck for whatever he did.

"Turn here," he ordered, gesturing down a long, dead-end dirt road she was familiar with. The road had a pasture on one side and trees lining the other.

She did as she was told and drove until

he told her to stop. She put the van in park, and he yanked her out of the driver's seat and into the back. He unlocked the door and yanked it open with the gun still pointed at her.

"Let's go."

"Where to?" she asked as she stepped out, looking around to see where she might run to safety.

He pressed her back to his chest and grabbed her around the throat. "Don't try anything stupid."

Her heart hammered in her chest. The pen in her back pocket was the only weapon of defense. She reached between them and cupped his crotch. "I'm willing."

He groaned and shifted his pelvis against her hand. She moved her other hand between them and eased the pen out of her pocket.

"You don't have a choice."

She turned in his arms and unbuttoned his jeans. When he didn't make a move to stop her, she held in her smile and slipped his zipper down. "I secretly always wanted you to be my first."

She flicked the cap of the pen to the left

as she cupped his balls in her other hand. She kissed a slow path up his chest to his neck. "I've wanted to do this for a long time," she whispered against his skin. She plunged the knife into his neck and rolled out of his hold, scurrying to hide behind the hood of the van.

Trent grabbed the knife and pulled it out, blood spurted from his neck as he turned to look at her. She could see the life in his eyes start to drain. "You bitch."

He raised the gun in her direction while she held her breath, hoping that the paralyzing agent or poison or whatever the hell was on the end of the blade went to work.

Gunshots rang out from the woods, and she peered around the van to find Trent lying on his stomach, the gun in the dirt and out of reach. Aiden stepped out of the trees.

"Are you okay?"

She nodded as she let the first of many tears slip free while rushing into his arms. He cradled her head against his chest as the sobs ripped free. "He shot my grandmother."

"Suzie has her in route to the hospital and under guard." He leaned out of the embrace and looked into her eyes. "Did he hurt you?"

She shook her head when Aiden's gaze turned to her neck where Trent had bitten her. He eased her shirt back. Anger stirred in his eyes as he looked back into hers. "We'll get you checked out at the hospital."

She nodded. "What about him?"

"He's not going anywhere." Aiden took Amber's hand and started walking down the dirt road. "Feds will be here any minute. When I finally got a hold of Suzie, she told me what happened, and I explained the tracker." He glanced at her and smiled. "She's tracking the GPS on my cell phone so she knows exactly where to find him and backup is on the way."

"What about the warehouse?"

"Roman and the team are handling it while some of the other feds are rounding up the locals involved. If I had to guess, by the time they're done interrogating everyone, they'll have more than just your grandmother willing to be witnesses."

Amber let out a breath she didn't realize

she'd been holding when they reached the SUV. Aiden opened her door, only stopping to kiss her lips.

"How did you know I was in trouble?" she asked as he got in the SUV.

"We finally got a picture of Trent's visitors."

Her brows dipped in confusion. "Who?"

"Bree and Lawson." He glanced her way. "They helped him set this whole thing up, acting as a knight to come save your grandmother. They had to figure that it would be the only reason you'd come back to town."

15 CHAPTER

Amber held out a cup of coffee to her grandmother as Aiden rolled his bag to the door. The gunshot had merely been a flesh wound on her thigh. The only true words that had come out of Trent's mouth.

"Are you sure you don't want me to stay and help?"

"You've wasted enough time helping me." She smiled up at him.

"Grams." Aiden walked over to her and pressed a kiss to her palm. "Remember what the doctor said. No wild parties for you, young lady, and next time you find a young stud, I want his name so I can run a background check."

She smiled and pink colored her cheeks. "That won't work, dear." She winked back. "I like the bad boys. I'm not sure any of them will pass your test."

He kissed her cheek. "I'll be seeing ya."

"You better," she teased back as Aiden walked to the door and grabbed his bag. Amber followed him onto the porch, letting the screen door close behind them.

"Last chance." He pulled her into his arms.

"I think I'm going to stay here awhile." Amber looked back toward her Grams, the woman who'd raised her when she had no one else. "She needs me right now."

"What about your job?"

Amber shrugged. "I don't know, family leave I guess." Her brows dipped. "And if they deny that, since I'm so new on the job, I might have to find a new one when I get back." She gave him a sad smile. "Maybe I'll work in security."

He cupped her face. This was it. An unfamiliar feeling clenched his heart. He couldn't make her return. He wouldn't ask.

Not when her grandmother and she needed each other. He gave a slow nod of understanding and pressed his lips to hers once more. "I understand."

He caressed her face, memorizing the way she looked in that one minute. Not the Amber who was trying to prove herself, or the Amber who was scared of her stalker, but Amber, his Amber. He kissed her once more before dropping his hold and stilling the urge to drag her with him. He picked up his bag and stepped off the porch. He wouldn't make this any harder than it had to be. He opened the SUV door and turned to look at her. "You're going to be fine."

She smiled and leaned up against the railing. "So are you."

****

Aiden returned to work after debriefing Marshall and Sophie on what had happened. Relief filled Sophie's eyes when he'd explained that Trent was dead. A tear of joy slipped free, although she attributed it to pregnancy hormones. Roman and Beau had invited him for a poker night, which

Aiden declined. A month had passed, and his life returned to normal. His house was void and as sterile as the day he'd left it. His phone vibrated with a text, and renewed hope blossomed for the first time. Hope that it was Amber and she was ready to come home. He'd go get her without a second thought.

His hope deflated upon finding that the text was from Marshall.

Emergency...my house, ASAP.

Twenty minutes later, Aiden took off his rain-soaked jacket and shook it before ringing the bell.

"He's here," Aiden heard Marshall holler.

The door swung open. "My wife is pissed at you." Marshall shook his head and patted Aiden's back as he led him into the living room where Sophie was lying on the couch. "Time to man up."

"How come you haven't gone back for her? I still can't believe you left her there," Sophie said in a way only she could. She coated her aggravation with sugar and honey.

"If it makes you feel better, I left more than her there." Aiden's gaze softened as he moved to sit beside Sophie on the couch. He lifted her feet and placed them on his lap. "I left my heart."

Sophie laid a gentle palm on his arm. "Go bring her home."

"I can't." He shook his head and rested it against the cushion. "I can't pull her away from her grandma."

Marshall crossed the room and placed a kiss on Sophie's head. "Aiden, let me give you some advice."

Aiden raised his head.

"You once helped Sophie and me to see the error of our ways."

"Oh, I wasn't wrong, sweetie. You just have a selective memory." Sophie laughed, as did Aiden as he remembered, when early in their relationship, he'd handcuffed them together and told them to make up when things had gone south between the pair.

"Be that as it may, the words of wisdom stand true to this day." Marshall grinned. "I think you told us back then..." he glanced at Sophie, "...and correct me if I'm wrong, honey, but I seem to recall Aiden telling us that sometimes we all need a little help."

Marshall nodded toward the door right before the doorbell rang. "I think you have a visitor."

Aiden moved Sophie's feet and hurried to the door. He pulled it open, and his heart started beating again for the first time in a month. Amber stood on the stoop in clothes soaked from the afternoon rain, her hair plastered to her face and she was out of breath.

"Where's Sophie? Has she had the baby yet?" The words were a whisper between them.

"What? No," Aiden answered, pulling Amber into his arms, kissing her lips, savoring and remembering the feel of her skin. She melded into his body, just the way he remembered. He broke the kiss and held her gaze.

"I love you." The words were whispered between them. "I'm all in. The white picket fence, the two point five kids, and the lazy Sunday afternoons; I want it all, as long as it's with you."

She smiled. "It took you long enough."

Aiden tossed his head back and

laughed. "Is that right?"

She nodded. Her smile grew. "I love you too."

"Okay, now that's settled. We'll have to celebrate later." Sophie held her stomach and appeared in the hallway, Marshall holding on to her elbow with one hand and carrying her overnight baby bag in the other. "I think our little bundle of joy has decided to make her appearance." Sophie let out several quick breaths. She smiled and looked up at Marshall. "We need to hurry."

****

Amber stood outside the nursery, staring in at Gracie Mae swaddled in a pink blanket. Aiden stood behind her, his arms wrapped around her body. "You were right. She's a beautiful baby girl."

Amber turned in his arms and laced her hands around his neck. "I've missed you."

"Oh, honey, I've missed you too."

He cupped her cheek and kissed her.

"You two get a room. You're hogging the window," Roman said as Beau and he approached the window.

Aiden rested his arm over Amber's shoulder and pulled her closer into his side.

"Glad you're back," Roman winked. "Maybe things will get back to normal."

"Uh...about that." Amber hesitated and glanced up at Aiden. "I'm afraid things have changed."

Aiden's brows dipped. "What changed?"

Marshall walked up to them and handed her a set of keys. "She's no longer working with Jack." He grinned. "She's working with us."

"Uh-huh." Aiden dropped his hold. "I won't have my future wife working missions."

"Future wife?" Amber grinned. "I don't recall you asking or me saying yes."

"Baby." He slid up to her and rested his palms on her hips. "You are going to marry me, aren't you?"

"That is so not the point," she answered and smiled. "You do realize that means giving up your bachelor pad and moving into my place? There's no way I'm living in that sterile house you call home."

"I don't care where we live, or how you

decorate, as long as we're together."

"I am working for Marshall." She smiled.

"We need to have a vote, so I'm afraid it's not official." He gave her a sly smile.

"All those in favor?" Marshall asked.

"Aye," they said in unison.

"Sophie agrees too." He patted Aiden on the back. "She's in. Trust me. You'll want her close by when working missions. I've learned that lesson the hard way."

"*She* is right here," she reminded them as Aiden pulled her into his arms and turned her to view the babies.

"I'll love you forever," he whispered into her ear and then kissed her cheek.

She gave him a sideways look and held his gaze. "And I'll love you back."

ABOUT THE AUTHOR

Kate has lived in Florida for most of her entire life. She enjoys a quiet life with her husband, Michael and two kids.

Kate has pulled all-nighters finishing her favorite books and also writing them. She says she'll sleep when she's dead or when her muse stops singing off key.

She loves creating worlds full of suspense, secrets, hunky men, kick ass heroines, steamy sex and oh yeah the love of a lifetime. Not to mention an occasional ghost and other supernatural talents thrown into the mix.